On a Rooftop in Beijing

Maggie Paredes

On a Rooftop in Beijing

This is a work of fiction. Any characters, businesses, places, events, and incidents are either the products of the author's imagination or used in a fictitious manner. Any resemblance to actual persons, living or dead, or actual events is purely coincidental.

Printed in the United States of America

Hardcover ISBN: 978-1-958714-35-5
Paperback ISBN: 978-1-958714-36-2
Ebook ISBN: 978-1-958714-37-9
Library of Congress Control Number:

MUSE LITERARY

CHICAGO·NEW YORK·PARIS·ROME

Muse Literary
3319 N. Cicero Avenue
Chicago IL 60641-9998

To all of the North Korean refugees
and those still stuck in North Korea –
I see you and will not forget you.

Author's Note

From 2008 until 2010, I lived in South Korea to teach English and plant a church with a Korean pastor. Never did I think I would be working with North Korean refugees while I was there, but that is what I ended up doing on the side.

About one year after arriving in the Chosun Dynasty, I was connected to some North Korean refugees through a pastor at a church. Shortly thereafter, I was able to hear the stories of plight that they shared – both publicly and in an intimate, small group environment. Their tales of horror while living in their home country of North Korea devastated me.

Upon learning of the realities that so many North Koreans face, I decided to join a group of people working to free them. These caring folks and I flew balloons full of food, South Korean newspapers, Bibles, and other items north in the hopes that many North Koreans would receive them. Also, we held rallies and prayer vigils about and for North Korea.

All of the names and the situations in this book are purely fictional. The plight of the North Koreans and the information surrounding that struggle is completely true, though, based on the knowledge that I received from North Korean refugees and those who help them.

The North Korean non-profit organization mentioned in this book has a purely fictional name. In addition, the parts about the American Embassy in Beijing in this book have been fictionalized by me.

In writing this book, my hope is not just to bring romance to the eyes, minds, and hearts of my readers but to open them up toward the conditions that the people of the Democratic Republic of Korea face.

If you find this book stirs your heart to help, here are some resources that you may use to jump in and serve:

PScore: http://pscore.org/about-us/

Crossing Borders NK: https://www.crossingbordersnk.org

Liberty in North Korea: https://www.libertyinnorthkorea.org

Helping Hands Korea: https://helpinghandskorea.org/.

Sloane
USA

Twelve years. That's how long it took me to make it to the Olympics. Twelve years of countless hours of swim practice. Twelve years of monotonous perfection of backstrokes, breaststrokes, butterflies, and freestyle swimming techniques so that I could try my best to win a gold medal. Twelve years of my coach barking orders at me so that I could become an aquatics machine.

My parents weren't Olympic swimmers or professionals, but they *were* athletes in high school and college, so I know that's where I get my determination and sporty drive.

Never did I think it would bring me to *him*, though. The one who changed my life, my world, and me, inside and out. When I finally reached my athletic awakening, I never imagined I would meet the one who would make my heart do the same open flips and turns I did every time I reached the end of one pool wall.

Neither did I believe that it would be almost impossible to be together. In actuality, I was naive about the mandates that his country put on him.

Would I change the way we met? Never for a day. Would I change his country? One hundred percent.

It all started with a look … one that would melt my heart forever.

Jae Sung (재성)
North Korea

My name means "rule." When my parents named me, I think they envisioned that I would take over the world like my home country's (North Korea) Supreme Leader, Kim Jong Il. However, they really named me after the South Korean actor, Choi Jae Sung, whom they watched illegally on a smuggled-in television under the covers of a blanket with all of the lights turned out at nighttime before I was born.

Like my parents, I have always been a rebel. The only thing that has kept me sane is swimming – when I feel the curve of the water lapping around my body, I feel as though I'm miles away from the poverty that my country sees on a daily basis. Miles away from the restrictions imposed on all of us who live in the DPRK. Miles away from the stress I feel to perform well, though by swimming, I *am* performing, if that makes sense.

Swimming saved me. It gave me the opportunity to attend the most prestigious high school in Pyongyang, the capital of my country and also my family's hometown. Without my swimming scholarship, I would not have been able to attend Kim Il Sung University, because my family is poor. Thank God I have good grades, often studying late into the night.

You would think that I would do better at school – my parents certainly hope that I would. Having their only son fail academically is such a shame on my whole family, and my dad makes that known every single day.

I wish my parents could see that swimming can take me places – even toward a coaching position, which is where my heart lies.

When North Korea was *finally* allowed to participate in the 2008 Olympics, I knew I had to jump on the chance to try to qualify. When you know you're good at something, you go after it – or, at least, that's what I've been taught.

So go after "it" I did … and much to my surprise (which it shouldn't have been), I got in! The team was so small (there were only five of us), so knowing that I could show the world that my country *does* have good people in it was a dream come true for me. The extra rations of rice for my family and for myself didn't hurt either. In fact, it filled our normally hungry stomachs.

When the day eventually came, when I got to walk across the ground floor of the 2008 Summer Olympics (based in Beijing, China), I was enthralled with all the different cultures and countries I saw – especially the USA.

I never knew that my dream would lead me to another dream – one that would burn the desire to be in a foreign swimmer's arms for the rest of my life.

I never knew that I would risk everything to be with this girl, even my life.

CHAPTER ONE

Sloane

Into the boisterous frying pan we go, I thought to myself as I made my way into the tunnel that would lead me and my fellow Team USA summer Olympics athletes into the procession of countries for what would be my first Olympics Opening Ceremony. *Be like Shirley Babanoff!*

Sloane, you ARE Shirley!

"Sloane!" my newest best friend, Grace, shouted, her green eyes lit up with enthusiasm similar to mine. "You need to fix your hat! It's crooked!"

Grace reached over and gently adjusted my Team USA cap so that it aligned with my field of vision.

"Thanks," I replied, feeling my grin grow. I couldn't believe I was here!

The Olympics! After two attempts since the age of thirteen to make the world competition, I was finally able to call myself an Olympian!

Though I had been swimming avidly since I was seven years old, I didn't try out for the world games until four years ago. This was a dream come true!

Grace was a marathon runner, which was like an unattainable goal to me. Running was something I could never do long-term (only for cross training) – but swimming. That. That was *everything* to me! Running wasn't my main sport.

There were American athletes from every state: Utah, New York, Texas, Florida, Louisiana, and more. We covered the entire nation. However, the athletes from other countries were the ones who intrigued me, especially the Asian ones.

I had never been one to travel abroad, but my heart ached for it. Ever since I saw the pictures of my older cousin Lesly's tour of Europe, I could feel the strings of longing tugging at my heart.

Although Lesly fancied navigating the Western hemisphere, I found myself drawn more to the Eastern side of the globe.

What was it about Japan, South Korea, and China that drew me in? I didn't know, but I definitely knew that I wanted to visit these three countries, specifically before attending Amherst College in just a couple of weeks, which was practically in my own backyard. Before being secluded in a place I knew so well, I wanted to see the world – namely, the region of Eastern Asia.

Well, after the Summer Olympics, of course.

The Olympics were held in Beijing this year, though, so I *was* hoping to get to see some sights on top of practicing and competing.

The noise level was growing, which indicated to me that it was almost time to step into the bright lights of the stadium.

"LET'S GO!!!!!!" shouted one American boy near me, thrusting his fist into the air, his face reddening.

This animalistic call led all of my fellow Americans around me to start shouting, "RED, WHITE, AND BLUE!" at the top of our lungs, and I found myself eagerly joining them. It was so easy to get pulled into the hype!

Before we stepped out of the tunnel, I took one look in the mirrors that lined the hallway. You know, just to make sure my hair was in place and my makeup wasn't smeared. Cameras would be everywhere, and I didn't want to find myself looking like a slob while representing my country. I could only imagine my mother's reaction to anything out of place on me: "Slooooane," she'd draw out my name, letting me know she was disappointed.

My copper-brown hair fell in curly waves to my shoulders, thanks to Grace's skilled hand. Not a string was out of place, but my tresses looked smooth and as ready as I was to get this party started. The pair of blue eyes peering back at me from the mirror, though – they were as scared as my soul felt about this tournament, ultra-wide with emotion.

It'll all be okay! All you gotta do is win gold, and you're home free. You've been doing this for so long that it's like second nature to you, I reminded myself securely.

There was a loud foghorn blast that signaled the time to walk out. We were one of the last teams to go, of course, as the countries came out region by region in alphabetical order. The wait time was a killer, but I spent the majority of it chatting with Grace and the other athletes around me. Luckily, they were just as nervous and elated as I was, so I felt a strong sense of camaraderie.

When it was finally time to go, we all marched through the double doors into a dimly lit stadium to the sound of almost deafening cheers from our parents and coaches –

"USA! USA! USA!" Our arms linked together like one big chain of unity.

Tears sprang to my eyes without my knowledge at the sound of the chants. I found myself waving like Miss America to the crowd, my hand bent into that crescent-moon shape that whoever the chosen one is always does.

Before I took my hand down, my vision caught the stare of a young Asian guy in a red track suit standing with the smallest team I had seen at the Olympics so far.

North Korea, I thought to myself. *Wow. I didn't know they were so hot!* At that thought, my face flushed. I wondered if Grace saw it.

By some miracle, North Korea had been allowed to compete in the Games this year. They had been vying for a chance to join the Olympics for years, but the Olympic Committee had always shot them down due to their human rights violations. This year, for whatever reason, they were given a chance – I found it odd that all of a sudden they were allowed to compete, but I wasn't in charge, so I guess it wasn't my business.

Despite my desire to look away, I just couldn't. As my eyes locked with his deep brown ones, his face started to beam as I felt a smile growing on my own, and it felt like a flower was opening up in my heart.

He sure is cute, I reflected. *I wonder if he can talk later.*

Chiding myself, I shook my head. *Sloane, you are here to win gold, not win the heart of some guy from a country run by a dictator. Plus, maybe he thinks American girls are easy.*

"Ugh! Watch out!" cried a fellow swimmer in front of me, Chloe, her face twisted up in disgust. She threw her coral-red hair over her shoulder.

"Sorry! I thought I saw someone I knew," I replied hastily, hoping that Chloe couldn't see my inflamed cheeks.

My new enemy responded by a look of annoyance. Great, I had made a foe at the Games now. Just another thing to worry about, huh?

Shrugging off my teammate's frustration and without a second glance toward this DPRK dream guy, I focused back on the cheering fans in the stands, which were too numerous to count.

When the American team reached the end of our walking area, we turned around and joined the giant circle with the other athletes from across the planet. In the middle of us was a stage where the Chinese performers would eventually be.

This was going to be an amazing time for sure! I tried so hard to capture this moment in my head, as I didn't believe in documenting every single thing on a phone. I wasn't your typical teenager I guess, because everywhere I looked, a kid my age would be on their phone or some other device, tapping away. My dad always said I was "old school," only using my phone if I absolutely needed it. Secretly, I bet he was happy about that – heck. I definitely saved him and my mom money!

Before the last country came out, I couldn't help but steer my vision over to the North Korean team again. It was like an invisible magnet was pulling my very spirit toward them.

Mr. North Korea was doing nothing else but gazing in my direction again!

I felt my heart start beating swiftly without asking me, threatening to jump out of my chest.

Uh-oh. This is going to be some big trouble, I warned myself.

I guess I was going to find out, *but how much trouble can you get in when you're with your coaches and teammates all day?*

CHAPTER TWO

Jae Sung (재성)

Deafening.

That is how I would describe the noise level in the Olympic Stadium. Everyone was so excited for the Parade of Nations, our voices rising and mingling in the air in different languages. All I could do was stand by with my North Korean teammates and watch all the countries walk by with fascination filling my soul. The athletes from the other countries all seemed to be in the same frenzy as I was – high on exhilaration in anticipation for the upcoming competitions.

Though we were only five people, the North Korean swim team was boisterous as well. Not only were we the only athletes from our country allowed to compete in the Olympics (no running, no volleyball, nothing else), we had pride, enough to make up for all of East Asia combined. And so we should – the Korean peninsula was established in 2,333 BC. Our region is one of the oldest in the world.

While North Korea has only been around since 1953 (following the Korean War), we have one of the strongest militaries in the world. Also, I was here at the Olympics to show these people that we were good at more than just flexing our soldier power.

I took a look down at my current team outfit – red, white, and blue. Only, our flag colors were much bolder than those of the American flags.

Tonight, my team and I were wearing navy blue bottoms and bright red hoodies with our red star in a white circle emblem on it.

The Supreme Leader met with us before our trip to China. I was so surprised by his unannounced visit to my home, just as much as my parents were. We rushed around to get him some tea and food.

"You must go before the foreigners and show them that North Korea is a strong, wonderful country," he advised me in a serious tone.

Though my parents couldn't hear it, I noticed an underlying, unspoken threat: ...*or else.*

It was not a secret that anyone who left our country to represent us and did not make North Korea proud while gone, any North Korean who did not agree with the Supreme Leader and our government, anyone who disobeyed the Supreme Leader's orders or hoarded food rations or anything of the like, any of these people would be killed or placed in a concentration camp.

My journey to the world-renowned Olympics would be one that would mean risking my and my family's life – and I did not have the choice to back out.

Late at night, I would often discuss my concerns quietly with my older sister, Ji-Hye (지혜), as we lay in our separate spaces on the floor in our shared bedroom. Ji-Hye's name meant "wisdom," and she showed a great deal of intelligence and insight on more than one daily occasion.

"There is nothing you can do about it, Jae Sung," she chided me. "You must go and make the Supreme Leader and our people proud."

Even before going to the Olympics, I felt trapped. What was once my love (and had paved the way for me to get a full scholarship to Kim Il Sung University) had now morphed into what felt like a mandatory prison sentence, one that might end in me and maybe my family being issued a death penalty or a real prison sentence in a gulag (which is a concentration camp).

I had no choice but to swim my very best I ever had. My family's very existence depended on it.

What would it be like to be fully free? How would it feel to eat as much as you wanted, when you wanted to (as I learned from the outlawed American radio station I listened to sometimes on my smuggled radio with an antenna attached)?

What would it be like to fail at the Olympics and know you would be able to go back home without being put in a concentration camp or killed?

As I pondered this, my eyes caught those of an American goddess also wearing red, white, and blue, staring back at me. Her cobalt-blue stare poured into my soul, and I couldn't break away from her gaze. My eyes cemented on the girl's, and I fixated all of my attention equally on her.

Soft, full, pink lips. Hair the color of vibrant chocolate. Body like an immortal, sculpted in all of the right places.

I felt my cheeks burning red with embarrassment, and I felt just as bad for her as she collided with the person in front of her. If anyone saw me staring at an American girl, I was sure to be in trouble. Still, despite the lurking danger, I couldn't stop staring.

Uh-oh, I thought amusedly, not taking my eyes off of the girl. I nodded my head toward her as if to say hello, but she didn't respond at all. Just kept staring. *Maybe I have something on my face?*

Then, the girl's face did something I thought could never make it look more beautiful – she put a smile on it. Her lips stretched out and warmed up her whole complexion more than I thought possible.

Areumdapda, I thought. She was *gorgeous,* that was for sure!

It was then that I was so glad my high school taught English to all of us for all four years – it would help if I got the chance to talk to this girl.

Who am I kidding? I asked myself wistfully. *If I try to get near her, my minder will take note of that. Everything I do or say, he writes down to report to the Supreme Leader later.*

I knew right then that the Olympics would be about more than enjoying my sport and competing for survival. The challenge was on to meet this girl!

CHAPTER THREE

Sloane

Waves of water gushed around my ears as I swam laps in the Olympic-sized pool during the American's practice time. I let it fill my heart too – with the joy that it always does.

Even as I exercised in what should be one of the most cherished times of my life, I just could not stop my thoughts from drifting to the guy I saw at the Olympic Opening Ceremony. The North Korean man. Or was he my age, eighteen?

What would my parents say? Would they be upset if they found out I had a crush on a guy from another country, much less one that was said to be so antiquated and restrictive? Would they be upset if I wanted to talk to him, to get to know him? What if this disappointed them, since I was supposed to be here to win gold, not to win the heart of someone I obviously wanted to get to know more.

Would he even be able to talk to me? I knew that North Korea didn't exactly look upon Americans in an esteemed way, like many other countries did. What if this guy was not allowed to even get near me?

The thought of not being able to talk to this guy sent my mind into a panic. Without thinking, I forgot to do my turn at the end of the pool and for the first time in a long time, I hit my hand on the pool wall harder than I meant to as I attempted to do my turn.

"Ouch!" I cried out as I clung to the pool wall with my uninjured hand.

My coach, Susan, was talking to another coach (possibly one from the UK) when she noticed my painful moment. Quickly, she rushed to my side.

"Are you okay?" Susan inquired, taking my hand gently in hers and inspecting it with a meticulous eye.

"I think so," I replied, looking up in the stands wistfully as I bent my wrist back and forth to demonstrate that I was okay.

Susan must have said something because I could hear her speaking, but my attention was solely focused on the team that was sitting in the second row: The North Korean team. Mr. Hot Asian Guy was standing on his feet, looking right at me, concern stretched across his face.

Wow, I thought, *He doesn't even know me, yet he is obviously worried about me. Maybe the feeling is mutual?*

It didn't surprise me that the North Korean team was here to watch us, because Susan had prepared me by informing me that athletes from all of the other countries would come to our practices to see what "we were made of." Also, she said, they would be watching to see if there were any tricks they could glean from us. We, too, would need to do this – sometimes, the best way to learn about swimming is to watch other players.

What surprised me was how concerned this guy was for me. We didn't even know each other, hadn't had the chance to talk (yet), but it was like we had known each other forever. Just the simple looks we were able to give each other between yesterday and today conveyed so much.

"Earth to Sloane!" Susan called, with an anxious scowl stitched on her perfect, bow-shaped lips.

I was immediately awakened from my mesmerized stupor, and I turned my attention back to my dutiful coach. "Sorry," I mumbled feebly. "What did you say?"

Susan let out an exasperated sigh. Maybe she was under more pressure than me. "Girl, you have to get your mind in the right place. Stop staring at the competition like they're a piece of meat and start focusing on your swimming."

Immediately, I felt my cheeks burn bright with embarrassment. How did Susan know that I was thinking about someone up in the stands, other than my obvious, lingering stare up there?

"You're right," I acknowledged shamefully, looking down at my red, Team USA, one-piece swimsuit with guilt flooding my system. "Now, what were you saying?"

I expected Susan to sigh again, but instead, a smile stretched across her youthful-looking face. "I *said* it doesn't look like a sprain, thankfully," she reiterated to me. "However, I want you to focus. Drop whatever you are thinking of and place your mind and heart in these games. This is practice for a reason – work out the kinks so you'll be ready for the placement trials."

Susan was so right. A four-time gold medalist, this former swimmer-turned-coach knew what I needed to be doing to follow in her footsteps. Any advice she gave me was golden in itself.

Also, she was my chaperone here in China.

My mom and dad had given me a serious talk before I left about focusing on the Games and "minding" Susan (which made me feel more like five years old than seventeen). Sometimes, I felt like I was competing for my parents and my coach more than myself.

Brushing aside any and all feelings and thoughts of attraction toward the unknown fellow Olympian I felt creeping up in my heart and mind, I closed my eyes and thought of *why* I was here.

I had been swimming in a pool since I was five, but I had been on swim teams since I was seven. My mom used to refer to me as her own "Little Mermaid."

At six, my mom enrolled me in an exclusive children's swim team in my hometown, Cape Cod, Massachusetts. According to the rumors of our neighborhood, this swim team was known to have produced many Olympians and seasoned athletes who went on to get scholarships and join other professional swim teams around the United States.

My mom had dreams in mind for me from the very beginning. On the other hand, I think my dad secretly hoped I would become a doctor, like him. Therefore, it was my mother I worried most about disappointing.

With one more wistful glance back into the stands, my eyes caught those of my watching admirer. He gave me a small smile, much to my delight.

I couldn't break my gaze away, no matter how hard I tried. As I watched, Mr. Unknown nodded his head toward the bottom row of the stands. Next, he placed a white piece of paper on the ground right in front of seat number one.

Hmmm, what could that be? A love note? I wondered, a mischievous smile inching its way onto my face. I hadn't gotten one of those since last year from Kyle Hendrickson. *Dear Sloane…*

I nodded my head back at my new, secret friend to indicate that I had seen the note and would get to it.

Like the good girl that I am, I finished my last round of freestyle swim practice. Then, I looked around quickly before briskly walking toward the stands and the letter that was so obviously left for me.

With trembling and wet hands, I folded open the note and read the sentence written in seven words, some of them misspelled.

"Meet me on the rof at midnit," was penned out for me on the page. I understood it to mean that this guy wanted to meet me on the roof of – where? – at midnight.

The Olympic Village, dorm number four?

How would I even get up there? Was there a staircase? All I knew was that I took the elevator to my room after practice and that was all. Sometimes, my roommates (also from the American swim team) and I had been ordering in some carb-loading food before or after our practices. I'd never been to any other part of the Olympic Village, though. In fact, I didn't even know that all of the athletes were housed in one building.

Would I meet him? Was it safe? Meeting a random stranger on top of a very tall building when everyone else was asleep could cost me it all – Susan may send me home, I feared.

Even though the Games *had* been so important to me, I *had* to meet this guy. This back-and-forth staring contest couldn't keep going on. I *needed* to get to know him! Was it worth the cost? Could I have *both* the Olympics and him?

My mind already made up, I gathered my towel and bag from in front of the pool and headed to the showers, ready to get back to the dorms with more haste than I had ever had since arriving in China.

CHAPTER FOUR

Jae Sung (재성)

Splash! Sounds of waves caressing the walls of the Olympic pool rang in my ears as my teammates and I watched the American women's freestyle swim team practice.

I had convinced our coach, Mr. Kim, to allow us to come watch Team USA practice in the hopes of seeing the girl I could not stop thinking about. Mr. Kim, however, thought it was because I wanted to see what maneuvers they were doing that we could try.

She had not looked my way once. In fact, she did not even know I was watching. I couldn't help it – I could not stop thinking of her.

Last night, as my head hit the pillow, all that went through my mind was *her*. Where was she from in America? I had not studied American geography much, but that was something I always wanted to do.

According to the Supreme Leader, it was good to know what America was like, in case we take over the country one day.

Maldo andoeneun, I thought with a shake of my head. There was *no way* we would take over America – nor could we. If my minder or my parents overheard the things I thought about our country alone in my head, I would be in trouble for sure. Not even they could protect me from our government's wrath.

To be honest, I did not agree with ninety-nine percent of what our country's leaders did or said. No, make that one hundred percent! I knew that their chief goal was to brainwash all of us into thinking that the Western civilization was out to get us, that they only wanted harm for us.

Now, being here at the Olympics, I could see that that was not the case. While many athletes from other countries eyed us suspiciously, I could tell it was more from curiosity than animosity. They wanted to know what we were like – maybe they were told the exact same thing we were? Perhaps they were told by their countries that we wanted to harm them, that we were out to get them, too.

Lost in my thoughts, I did not notice that my new, favorite American athlete had hurt herself until I heard her cry out.

"Ouch!" she cried as her hand ran into the wall. Immediately, she sprang up from the water and balanced herself on the wall with her good hand.

Without thinking, I was on my feet, feeling helpless and wanting to intervene, to render some help. What could I do, though? I could not go down to the pool to give her some aid without my minder taking note and without a sure reprimand if not something more dangerous.

I stole a nervous glance in the direction of my minder, Byung Hun. Sadly, he had noticed that I jumped up, so I let him know that I was merely standing to stretch my legs. He acknowledged my response with a nod of his head.

Thankfully, someone came up and crouched down by the pool, examining the girl's hand.

Kochi, I surmised to myself. She must be her coach.

While this beautiful girl's coach helped her out, I stood by and watched forlornly, my lovesick heart thumping wildly in my chest.

Shockingly, the girl looked up in the stands.

It was as if she was looking to see if I was there. There I was. My heart felt so connected to her, more than any person I had ever felt an attraction to before.

There had been Su Jin in my second year of high school at Ansan High School. We would sneak to the art room during lunch to kiss. If anyone ever knew, I would surely be reprimanded in some way, and it would not be good for my family and I. Surprisingly, my time with Su Jin ended when the art teacher stumbled upon us one day, her face looking flustered, then morphing into one of disgust.

"Agdandeul!" she screamed at us angrily. "What do you think you are here for? This is not the place or time to be kissing! You are at school – study only! Get out of here!"

I thought for sure that Su Jin and I would be called to the Juyohan's office that very day, but I was thankfully wrong. However, I never met with Su Jin again, for fear that both of us would get in trouble. We would pass each other in the halls, shooting each other a painful look of desire, but nothing more.

My fellow Olympian and I continued to stare at each other as I could feel the gaze of our team's minder trained on my face.

"Anja," he ordered. I wanted to sit down, but I could not.

The practice ended abruptly anyway, so my team, our coach, and our minder all got to their feet with me. As we began to make our way to the stairs to exit the stands, I allowed everyone to go in front of me so that I could do what I really came here for.

Shaking, I nodded my head toward the first row of the stands so that Ms. America could see.

Then, I placed the note I had written for her on the tier's floor.

Had she seen it? Yes, she had. She nodded back at me, and I knew she would get the note.

A feeling of fright shot through my veins like ice water going down my throat. Had my minder seen? I looked up ahead of me at my group, which was at least three feet in front of me.

Thankfully, no one had looked back at me! Yes! Honorably, I followed my fellow North Koreans toward the exit, my heart jumping around in my chest.

If everything went according to plan, I would be meeting this girl I could not get out of my mind within five hours on the top of our current living quarters. Life could not get better than this!

CHAPTER FIVE

Sloane

Darkness. That's what surrounded me like a cloak as I climbed the ten flights of stairs from the tenth floor (where I was staying with my fellow American swimmers) to the rooftop. The only thing paving a pathway of light for me was my iPhone, which I kept trained in front of me.

This was crazy. What was I thinking? What would my mom and dad say? What would Susan do if she found out what I was doing?

Yet, I couldn't stop. I couldn't turn back now.

All I knew was that I had to meet this guy! If I never did, it would haunt me for the rest of my life, that was a fact.

Would I regret this night? I didn't know. What I *did* know was that I was not going to stop until I met the one who drew my focus away from the gold medal.

After I had left the pool, the image of Mr. Unknown flashed in my mind what seemed like a thousand times, again and again. Instead of photos of swimming techniques wading through my thoughts, pictures of his eyes floated in front of my face. I couldn't get the sizzling way we had connected out of my mind.

A sheer curiosity and desire drove me on, step by step.

If only I could take this desire and channel it into my swimming this week, like I am supposed to, I reprimanded myself, silently pleading with my heart to let me get back to my sport tomorrow.

There was only *one more day* to practice.

That's all. After that, it was all or nothing. Therefore, I had no time to play. Yet, here I was – as if an unseen force was driving me on, I was making my way to what could potentially threaten my future as an athlete rather than flourish it.

If I was going to go down for something, I guess it should be for a chance to meet this guy who had attracted me more than any other, right?

And here I was…at the very top step of the stairs, the brown door looming in front of me. The guy who would no longer be a stranger might be on the other side of the door, waiting for me.

My heart sped up what seemed like a thousand beats per minute, threatening to jump out of my chest. Taking a deep breath, I slowly inhaled and exhaled.

One last look at myself, I decided, turning my iPhone's camera on so I could check out my brunette tresses in its reflection.

My hair had been dry for hours since swimming, but it hung in wavy strings to my shoulders. "I should've run a brush through this mangy thing," I muttered out loud to myself.

Oh well…I am who I am. He either likes me or he doesn't. It seems like he already does, judging by the looks he's been giving me.

That last thought brought a quick smile to my face and melted away some of my nerves.

With a shaky hand, I turned the doorknob and opened the door. I didn't know what to expect on the other side – would it be dark on the roof or light? Would we have to sit on the floor or would there be chairs? What would we talk about? Could he speak English? Should I try to learn Korean so we could communicate?

Taking another deep breath, I stepped onto the roof. Peering around, I spotted Mr. Unknown at the far-right corner of the roof, peering out into the city lights of Beijing.

I took the time to study his features from behind. He had a nice butt, that was for sure.

Judging by his behind, he was definitely a swimmer, like me. Since the North Koreans brought eleven teams this year, I didn't know if he was a competing athlete or a coach or what. If he was an athlete, what sport did he play? Was he a swimmer, like me?

My feet crunched on some rocks on the roof, signaling to Mr. Cutie that I had arrived. Swiftly, he turned around with a serious look on his face, and I thought he was going to tell me that he didn't want to see me after all. Instead, a smile that matched mine broke out on his olive skin.

"Hello," he said simply, quietly.

I strained to hear him speak, wanting to learn every tone his voice made. His voice was low and smooth, like butter to my ears.

"Hi," I answered back, feeling suddenly shy, my eyes wandering downward to look at my black and white Converse-clad feet.

Without my body knowing what it was doing, I closed the gap between us, almost running toward the guy. I couldn't get there fast enough. My hands were slick with sweat, so I wiped them down on my ripped blue jeans.

"I'm Sloane," I offered my new friend (or whatever you would call him).

"I am Jae Sung," he replied, stepping closer to me.

Jae Sung, I rolled the name around in my head. What did it mean? I had never known anyone from Korea before – North or South. Even at my high school, there were no Korean students. Therefore, this name was new to me.

"What does Jae Sung mean?" I asked timidly, drawing closer to him with a little step in his direction.

He stepped closer to me too, never taking his eyes off of me. I could see them burning with a desire to get to know me, just like my soul was yearning to know him better too. His face was a mask of confidence and earnestness as he stared at me once more.

"It means honest, or sincere," he informed me. "What does Sloane mean?"

"I don't know," I answered truthfully. "It was my grandma's maiden name."

A smile broke out on Jae Sung's full lips, lightening up his serious facial expression a bit. "I like tradition," he let me know with a zealous reach for my hand.

That made me smile back. My family has always been quite traditional. I wasn't *that* aware of the North Korean family culture, but I was willing to bet anything that it was traditional as well, as many East Asian cultures are.

Without a second thought, I took his hand in mine. His fingers wrapped around mine immediately. It felt natural, not at all strange. This person that I had known for all of five minutes or less felt like *home* to me, surprisingly.

"Want to sit over there?" Jae Sung gestured to a comfortable looking, red and yellow-striped couch tucked in the corner of the roof, a vibrant emerald green plant spilling its leaves out over it like a protective umbrella.

I hadn't noticed *that* before, maybe because my mind was just too focused on getting close to him. Nodding vehemently, I agreed, "Sure."

There was so much I wanted to know about Jae Sung, so much I wanted to ask. I was scared, though – I didn't want to come off as too eager.

Would he judge me for being excited though? We were already holding hands, which was a pivotal step in the direction of a relationship.

Jae Sung sat down meekly next to me, and I noticed that our thighs touched. I could feel his strong leg muscle through his jeans, and I felt my pulse quickening. Even though I had seen cars out on the road, all I could hear was Jae Sung's voice. Even though a wind had started blowing softly against my skin, all I could feel was his leg against mine, warm and inviting. My senses were numb to everything but Jae Sung.

He smelled like my favorite odor – the pool. I'm sure I smelled like that too. We were two people who spent most of our lives in the water. Trying not to appear nervous, I turned my body so that I was facing him directly.

"How do you know so much English?" I asked, leaning toward him with curiosity written all over my face.

I expected this question to take him aback, but it didn't. Instead, he replied, "We had to take English all four years at my high school in Pyongyang."

"We only had to take two years of a language at my high school," I retorted. "Usually, it's just Chinese, German, Spanish or French. I took Chinese because I'm interested in Asia."

Our conversation went back and forth like this, as if we were working on piecing together a puzzle. Time felt like it stood still.

We both weren't even aware that a couple of hours had passed by until Jae Sung suddenly said, "Aaaassssh," glancing at his titanium silver watch with a look of frustration.

I didn't know what "Aaaasssh" meant, but based on Jae Sung's anguished-sounding response, I could tell it wasn't good. Patiently, I waited for him to tell me, but I was eager to know what was going on in his mind right now. Heck, all the time since I had seen him at the opening ceremony two days ago if I was being honest.

"I must return to my room. It is already 2:00 a.m.! My minder wakes up in the middle of the night to go to the restroom," he let me know, a sheepish look on his face. "I hope he did not get up already and find me gone."

"Minder?" I pondered curiously, my brown eyebrows nearly touching the hairline on my forehead. "What's that?"

Jae Sung got up quickly so I did too, but I wanted to know what a "minder" was before we left. Touching his arm, I waited for his response.

"It is someone who watches me. They are sent by the government with anyone who leaves our country," he responded without a hint of concern in his voice. In fact, he sounded neutral, like this was normal.

I did my best to hide my shock. "Oooooh," was all I said as I stopped at the door, not wanting this night to end. What would someone see if they watched me all the time? Honestly, I couldn't imagine being patrolled like a hostage when I was in another country. This time was supposed to be one of fun and accomplishment, not captivity. *Fun* was what I would give Jae Sung while we were here, I decided right then and there. If I could improve his time away from North Korea, I would work hard to do so! It didn't hurt that he was attractive, either.

"This was so good," Jae Sung whispered to me, his face beaming.

I did my best to commit his face and body to memory – in case things got busy, and I didn't see him again. Square jaw line, rounded nose, big brown eyes the color of a murky lake, thick eyebrows that looked good on him (surprisingly). As for his body – wow! I tried not to appear too enthralled by its strong physique. Jae Sung's muscles showed in all of the right places. I wouldn't mind looking at him all day!

"Definitely," I acknowledged his sentiment with a small smile. "We should meet again some time."

Nodding, Jae Sung countered, "My minder goes to bed at around 11:30 p.m. Do you want to meet me here every night at midnight?"

My heartbeat stepped it up a notch. Every night in China with Jae Sung on the roof? I couldn't think of anywhere else I would rather be while I was at the Olympics! Yet, I was here for a gold medal. I was here to use all of my training to the best of my ability. My heart was torn into two pieces. What should I do?

Shaking the doubt from my mind, I gave Jae Sung a "yes." I decided that I would scream "YES" off the balcony if I could! This was the best thing to ever happen to me besides the Olympics!

"Tomorrow then," he replied to me, leaning in.

I held my breath. *This is it,* I thought, *A kiss.*

Closing my eyes, I leaned my head forward...only to meet Jae Sung's shoulder as he wrapped me in a tight embrace.

Well, that's better than nothing, I decided, my hope wavering.

Before he opened the door and disappeared into the dark stairwell, I gave Jae Sung one more smile and a wave. He quickly did the same.

*A minder....*What had I gotten myself into?

CHAPTER SIX

Jae Sung (재성)
Two Weeks Ago

All of the North Korean athletes sat still in the room on the fourth floor of the Blue House, waiting for the Supreme Leader's arrival. We were told he had an important message for us, one that would encourage us before we drove to Beijing.

When Kim Jung Il entered, he was flanked by a multitude of personnel – a bodyguard, soldiers (most of whom looked like high-ranking officials, judging by the number of badges on their uniforms), and men in suits that I couldn't quite place.

Everyone stood to their feet when he entered, and we bowed deeply, not putting our eyes on the Supreme Leader out of respect (and admittedly: fear).

"You may be seated," Kim Jung Il commanded in Korean, his booming voice sounding like the words of a judge in a courtroom. "Thank you for joining me here today, *dongji*."

Comrades. As if we were all a part of one big army. Yes, I would have to go to the army for two years at some point before the age of twenty-five, but all of the men and women of my country were considered a part of the government's task force.

"I have some very important things to tell you, to remind you of your course," the Supreme Leader informed us.

His eyes trained on all of us in the room, stopping to rest on mine. I tried my best not to squirm in my seat, my hands immediately sprouting sweat like a sprinkler. To hide my trepidation, I put my hands in my lap and warned myself not to look at the ruling *Seongsangnim*.

"When you go to the Olympics, you will be looked at quite a bit. You *are* from the greatest land in the world, after all. In addition, you *may* be spoken to by the people of the countries that are inferior to ours, which would be all of them."

What was this about? What was the Supreme Leader going to challenge us to? My head swam with ideas as I trained my vision on an ant crawling across the concrete floor.

"If you speak to someone from another nation, if you look at them, your minder will let me know, and you will be punished severely when you return to North Korea. *If* you return," Kim Jung Il threatened, his voice taking on an even more serious tone (if that was even possible).

My heart sped up involuntarily in my chest, and a cold sweat of fear broke out all over me. What did *punishment* mean? Would we be sent to a prison camp, killed, or not allowed to return home but banished to live in another country?

"The Americans and those of the Western countries do not like us. They never have and never will. Also, they want to *be* us. Any information we give them about ourselves and our country will only end in utter destruction for us. Their minds are lowly and only think about things that can defeat us, bring us down."

Was that true? I found myself questioning the Supreme Leader without reserve. Shaking my head, I was determined to believe my leader. There was a reason he was in charge, there was a reason that his father, the Great Leader Comrade (may he rest in peace) felt the need to assign his son as the next chief in place of our great land.

"They will tell you lies, and spread blasphemous falsities about all of us here in the great nation of North Korea. You must not listen. Be determined when you go to the Olympics that your only course of action is to win a medal for this country and bring glory and honor to not only me and this land, but your families," Kim Jung Il continued, his message changing to a more inspirational tone.

Just when I thought the Supreme Leader had finished up his directive toward us, he ended on this ominous note: "And be sure of this – if you come back here without a medal, if you engage with a foreigner, you will not face a favorable return."

I swallowed down the lump that had formed in my throat, forcing myself to breathe in and out slowly. If Kim Jung Il was threatening us like this about our time at the Olympics, what would he think of the illegal devices my family and I secretly used on a regular basis? What about my grandmother, who was a Christian? If the Supreme Leader discovered this hidden fact, would he punish me and my family? I had heard stories of Christians being sent off to prison camps or killed in public executions. What would become of my family?

I knew right then that my only choice was to go to the Olympics and keep my eyes focused on the prize: A medal. It was all or nothing.

CHAPTER SEVEN

Sloane Two Weeks Ago

Being an only child was not something I took lightly. All of my parents' hopes and dreams for their offspring's success was on *my* shoulders.

While my dad wanted me to graduate from high school and begin the long trek to medical school, my mom supported whatever dreams I had. It was always a source of contention between the two of them.

It was only inevitable, then, that when I qualified for the Olympics in the swimming pre-trials, my parents displayed different reactions to my personal athletic achievement. My mom jumped for joy in the stands (according to my best friend since kindergarten, Ava, who traveled to the trials with us). On the other hand, my dad just sat there, solemn, showing no enthusiasm on his tight-lipped face.

Instead of working on my own body, he wished for me to work on other's bodies. This wasn't my calling, this wasn't what I wanted, but I couldn't quite tell him yet. How could you crush your father's dreams when you were an only child? There were no other kids for my dad to put his goals onto.

As I packed, my mom sat on the purple desk chair that matched the thick duvet on my queen-sized bed. She had her legs crossed and was swinging her right foot in circles lazily.

If you first glanced at my mom, she looked to be an older sister rather than my mother. It was everything I could wish for that I would look like her when I got older. Her bright eyes, wide without a single wrinkle or blemish.

My parents had always called for perfection – and I tried my best to give it.

"Remember to follow your coach's directions. Don't talk to people you don't know, as exciting as that may seem. Also, try to stay with the American group if you go anywhere – don't stray away from them," my mom rattled off an endless list of reminders.

Rolling my eyes, I gave in to my mom's fears and replied, "Yes, Mom."

My dad peeked his head in the door, his brunette silver-streaked hair flashing in the lamp-light. "Get through this round of the Olympics and when you come back, you'll be ready to start your journey to follow in my footsteps as a doctor."

My heart thudded in my chest. How could I tell my dad that I didn't *want* to be a doctor? That I didn't quite know *what* I wanted to be "when I grew up?" All I had ever wanted was to swim, and I was doing that.

According to my dad, though, "swimming was not a job." I wanted to remind him of the swimming instructors at the YMCA, the coaches who helped bring people to a peak performance, the money that a gold medal from the Olympics would bring…but I just kept my mouth shut when he rambled on about "getting this out of my system and moving on."

I knew there *had* to be resentment between my mom and dad because it was my mom's idea to get me into swimming in the first place. She was the one who saw the spark in me and allowed me to go for it. There was a little bit of guilt on my part because of that.

"Dad," I whispered, my throat constricting as I tried to force the words out, "I don't want to be a doctor. In fact, I don't know *what* I want to be just yet."

My dad's brown eyes grew wide with concern and his face contorted into a worried scowl. "You will need to figure that out soon," he retorted, "because you start college in the fall. However, we have had this discussion many times, Sloane."

I swallowed the lump in my throat, fighting back the tears that sprang to my eyes. What more could I say? He would never listen. *It might be best to just agree with him now and do what I want,* I decided silently.

Mom stayed quiet, but her leg circling stopped. She sat as still as a mouse on the bed, suddenly sitting upright.

Maybe they would not last another five years, I thought in a panic. Would my choices break their marriage up?

Dad stood there awkwardly, wordlessly beckoning for a reply from me, but I didn't give it to him. I just continued to place my endless supply of Team USA gear into my silver hardcover suitcase.

Without saying anything else, he briskly walked out of the room, and Mom let out a deep breath. I didn't realize she was holding her breath until now.

"You do you, Sloane," she admonished me. "You're a capable, smart, talented young lady who is becoming a woman of strength and integrity. I trust whatever you decide."

Hearing these words from my mother meant *the world* to me. Why couldn't my father trust me to make the right decisions for myself too? Wishing for that day may never come.

I felt my dreams of getting my dad's approval die right then and there. To be honest, I felt a little lighter when I let go of his expectations for me. I could never meet them, so why try?

There had been that time during my sophomore year that I dated Jake Cunningham, a football player at my high school. Jake was a senior, which automatically qualified him for my dad's disapproval. When I started to go out with him in his shiny Trans Am, my dad put his foot down.

Within a week, I had reluctantly broken up with Jake. Like a sad little puppy, I had followed my dad's orders.

The day I qualified for the Olympics, something changed in me. I was no longer willing to follow my dad's plans to the T.

Now, as I was packing, I decided to start living *for myself.* What were *my* dreams and *my* goals? Beijing was going to be the start of *my* plans, I resolved. Who I dated, where I went to college, what I studied, and what I wanted to do with my life would be *up to me.*

Whether my dad liked it or not, I was going to be making my *own* decisions from now on. I was eighteen, after all.

CHAPTER EIGHT

Jae Sung (재성)
Today

A million lights, spread out over the whole city, greeted my vision as I leaned on the balcony on my elbows, my head splayed in my hands. Back home in North Korea, it was so dark at night. Even though lights were turned out early in the night due to government orders, and people hid under their blankets and such so that they could listen to illegal radio or watch forbidden, foreign TV shows, flashlights blazing.

This. This was something spectacular that I had never seen before! Before coming to China, I had done my research on the smuggled laptop I'd bought on the black market. I figured since this might be my only chance to leave North Korea, it would be best to get to know the country I was visiting.

Unlike my home nation, the nation of China was allowed to watch TV and listen to music that was not about their leader. They even listened to and watched these things for fun! The very thought of that shocked me to the core.

This made me think about the American girl I would be meeting tonight. What kind of life did she live in the United States? Was she allowed to watch anything on TV or listen to music? What was American television and music like? Though I had been studying English in high school, we were told that the citizens of the USA were all entitled, thought they owned the whole world, and that they wanted to be like us in North Korea. Was this all true?

My *halmeoni* (grandmother) told me when I was very young that I was so curious that it would get me into trouble one day. Was that a premonition? Would I be shipped back to North Korea in a body bag because of my simple desire to get to know a girl?

Halmeoni also let me know that I would change the world. All I wanted to do was change the world of my family – a gold medal was rumored to be worth thirty-seven thousand dollars! What I could do with that to change my family's life.

Here I was, thinking about meeting a girl, when I should be focused on my family. My heart and mind were conflicted: one said, "Focus on your swimming," while the other said, "Focus on this girl whom you cannot stop thinking about." Which should I listen to?

Abruptly, I was startled from my thoughts when the door to the roof came open. For a moment, I worried that it would be my minder. *Has Byung Hun woken up?* What would happen to me if he found me out here alone and not in the bed (where I was pretending to be asleep) when he announced lights out for the swim team he was in charge of?

"Hello," I greeted this girl that was in my heart and mind so deeply.

Hello? I chastised myself silently. *What kind of greeting is that? I should have said, "Hey there," which is something I read Americans say to each other when they greet one another.*

"Hi," the girl responded, her brown hair hanging in what looked like mahogany strands of a magical tree hanging to her back.

Shocked, I watched the American girl walk toward me, step by step. She seemed unsure of herself – just like I did. However, I wanted to appear confident, so I stood up straight and made my face levelheaded.

"I'm Sloane," she said, her voice sounding like water running gently through rocks in a stream.

"I am Jae Sung," was all I could manage to say before I needed to swallow a little. I could feel my heart practically jumping into my throat with nervous energy.

She was full of questions, for she asked me what my name meant next. It was cute, her desire to know me more intimately, starting with my name.

I let her know that my name means *honesty* or *sincerity*. In my country, we believe that names predict who or what a person will be. Hal Albeoji (Grandfather) wanted me to be a person of truth, so he led my parents to the right name for me. In all that I am today, I try to live up to the name and the reputation that my halbeoji had for me.

Though he is no longer with us, my abeoji still impacts my family today. Any time we would make a mistake when we were little, Ji-Hye would whisper to me, "*I munjeleul haegyeolhalyeogo habnida. Abeoji jalangseuleobge mandeulgo sipseubnida.*" ("Let's try to fix this. We want to make Grandfather proud.")

Being the only boy in my family also required more from me than my sister, though she was older than me. I would carry on the family name, so I had to make sure that I would do so in a good manner, not bringing shame to anyone.

Despite my desire, I could not help but think about how my parents would be disappointed in me right now: up on a roof in the middle of the night with an American girl.

Pushing that thought out of my mind, I took Sloane's hand without a second thought and suggested that we sit on the little couch in the corner of the roof.

I just wanted to be close to her, that was all I wished for. Never mind my family right now. Never mind my minder, the Supreme Leader, my obligations at the Olympics to bring honor and glory to my country. I was here with Sloane right now, and that was all that mattered to me.

As we sat down, our legs touched. I could feel my knee warming up with the sensation, and I chose not to move from this position. Before we spoke, I took a brief moment to look at her more closely. Square jaw, pointed and petite nose, round, blue eyes as deep as the Korean Sea, chestnut-brown hair parted down the middle that appeared so soft. Her features were delicate yet held a sense of prestige and poise.

We talked about our language abilities, which was a very intriguing topic for me.

Interestingly, I wanted to know more about American life. What was high school like there for the kids my age? It was surprising to me that the upper grade students were *allowed* to choose which language they would like to learn, instead of being *told* which language they must acquire.

The time did not feel like anything when I was with her on top of the swimmer's building. I did not want the time to end, but I quickly snuck a glance at my watch and nearly jumped up with fright when I realized it had been *two hours* since we joined each other tonight! I had to go or I would be found out, for sure. My minder *always* got up to use the restroom some time in the night.

Chills went through my body as I realized my minder could have gotten up and realized I was not already there. My mind raced through the possible scenarios: Byung Hun could be looking for me right now, knocking on every door, waking everyone up, making a note to talk to the Supreme Leader about my poor behavior!

"I must return to my room. It is already 2:00 a.m.! My minder wakes up in the middle of the night to go to the restroom," my mouth mumbled, hoping that Sloane did not think I was weird for having a minder. "I do not want him to get up and find me gone."

She hastily asked me what a minder was and I let her know the truth. My name was not *Jae Sung* for anything! I had no problem with sharing the truth no matter the cost. Also, my heart told me that this girl would not judge me for having a minder.

Instead, Sloane let out an "Ooooooh," in a song-like voice. I could not tell if this was good or bad, as I had never encountered a reply like this before. However, I chose to believe that this was just a neutral reaction.

"This was so good," I whispered to Sloane, leaning forward. My lips begged for me to kiss her, but I would not. It would not be honorable this first night.

She recommended that we meet again, and I agreed with a definite nod of my head. I let her know the time that my minder went to bed and suggested that we meet at midnight every night.

Tomorrow was another practice. Three more days of practice until the Olympic games began, in fact. This would give me three nights with Sloane. It was not much, but I would take all I could get just to be near her for as much time as possible.

"Tomorrow then," I confirmed, leaning even closer toward her. My body felt drawn to hers like a magnet. Wrapping an arm around her, I pulled Sloane into a close hug. Every curve of her body molded into mine like glue. I did not want to move, but I knew that I would have to if I did not want to encounter any involuntary trouble from my body.

Sloane waved good-bye to me and smiled at me, and I returned the gesture as I opened the door and started the descent down the stairs to my room.

Getting in trouble is worth it for her, I thought to myself, a smile that I could not contain stretching across my lips, my heart burning inside of my chest with joy.

CHAPTER NINE

Sloane
Today

"**U**SA! USA! USA!" The chants would be thunderous in my ears if it weren't for the water in the Olympic swimming pool lapping my ears.

Another practice day was almost in the books, and I felt completely strong. I knew that I was ready for the Olympics already.

It was the day after meeting Jae Sung...the day after an epic time. This was more than just "adding one more thing to my bucket list." Oh, I met a North Korean. Oh, I met a cute guy from a different country. This felt like a life-changing moment for me.

Swimming in the lane to my right of me was Natalie Coughlin, a swimmer from California. On my left was Dara Torres, also from California. What was it with these West Coast girls? They were all like mermaids in the water, natural born swimmers with feet for flippers. I would have to show them that an East Coast girl could do as much damage in the pool as they could!

Yes, we were on the same team. Even still, we were all competing for the gold – I reminded myself.

Natalie took a deep breath as she came out of the water and bobbed up and down next to me, her hand gripping the edge of the wall like mine. "How do you feel about your practices?"

If I were honest with her, my head wasn't fully in the game; neither was my heart. Both my thoughts and my feelings were with Jae Sung. It was a strange sense – I came here for a gold medal, yet I felt as though I was competing to win the heart of a guy I had just met.

All of my life, I had been trained for this moment: A chance to compete in the Olympics. Just once would be a dream come true. When I beat Kara Lynn Joyce by literally five seconds, thus securing my spot on the Olympic women's swim team, I could hear my mom shouting so loudly from the stands that I thought an earthquake was happening. I needed to look at the replay on the giant TV screen to make sure I had really beat her. When I discovered that I had, I almost couldn't believe it. Shock ran through me, inside and out.

You train your body like it's your work horse, you eat nothing but the healthiest of food, you replay moments where you could have done better at your practices. All of it comes down to the moment you are able to say, "I am an Olympian."

So what makes Jae Sung so special? Why does my soul feel like it's connected to him and what is it that makes me feel like I *have* to get to know him, perhaps risking my chance at winning gold?

"Hello?" Natalie interrupted my deep thoughts, waving her hand in front of my eyes, an amused smile playing on her lips. "Earth to Sloane! Are you there?"

"Sorry. I was just thinking about how amazing it is to be here!" I hastily replied. "My practices? Oh, they've been good. My body feels ready – but my mind isn't."

Natalie nodded energetically, her red and white Team USA cap allowing a few strands of brown hair to peek out around her ears. "You have to remind yourself of why you came, what you're doing it for. Don't lose sight of your *reason* to stay in the game."

Something told me to listen to this girl that I barely knew. Natalie seemed to have wisdom beyond her years.

I wish I could see Grace, but she was so busy practicing, just like me. If we were both swimmers, we could spend time together in the pool. However, her sport was one on the road while mine was one in the water. Maybe she would come watch me on my swim meet day? In turn, I could go watch her run her race.

Back in Cape Cod, I ran 5ks and 10ks in order to cross-train. I'd never run anything longer than a six-mile run, though. Half-marathon? You have to be kidding me! How do people even do a *full* marathon, either?!

I'm sure that Grace thought the same thing about swimming and me. While I could stroke back and forth in the pool for hours, Grace could probably hit the pavement for a long time, too.

"I'll keep that in mind. Thanks, Natalie," I offered a genuine smile.

It didn't slip my mind that this was my competition, too. Natalie was a fierce competitor, as I had seen in the Olympic pre-trials. In fact, she had set a record with a time of 53:39 at the Olympic trials back in Omaha, Nebraska. In contrast, my time was 54:51. While it was enough to earn me third place (just 5 seconds ahead of Dara Torres at 54:57), I saw how Natalie fought for her place in the 2008 Olympics. She fought with her very spirit, not just her body.

Did I still have that determination or was I just the same little girl swimming circles in the pool like I was in beginner's class? I would find out soon enough.

Something caught my eye in the stands. A North Korean jacket. A bunch of them, to be exact. This time, it looked like more than just the swimmers coming to watch the Americans practice.

In fact, it was the whole squad, no matter the sport. While they were a small number (maybe only about thirty people), it was enough to intimidate. Were they as good as us? That I would find out soon enough, too.

I searched for Jae Sung and found him almost immediately, his eyes trained on mine as well. We shared a smile, one that I frankly didn't care if Natalie or Susan or anyone else noticed.

Natalie followed my gaze up to the stands. Her eyes widened. "You have the hots for a North Korean swimmer? Ooooh, girl, be careful! You never know how *those* guys are!"

"What do you mean?" I queried, my heartbeat raising just a hair.

Natalie studied me like I was a little girl attending my very first day of school, a concerned look on her face that looked faker than the salon nails my arch-nemesis, Chloe, had on since day one.

"Sloane, they come from a patriarchal country. Do the math," she said before returning to her practice.

Patriarchal. Male-dominated. I wondered if Jae Sung's mother was treated well by her father? Did they raise him to be gentle and kind? I'd have to ask him about his family when we met tonight on the roof.

Before I returned to my practice, I noticed that Jae Sung dropped a tiny sliver of a note between his feet. He gestured downward toward the letter before he and his team got up to leave the stands.

The end of my practice couldn't finish enough! When Susan came over to talk to me about the plan tomorrow, I couldn't get her to shut up fast enough. I pranced from foot to foot like I had to pee, thinking maybe she would get the hint. Then, I raced to the stands to pick up the letter from my guy.

My wet fingers delicately unfolded the letter, and I took the words into my heart and mind as I read them silently to myself:

You look so byutiful today, Slown. I cannot wait to talk to you tonight, the letter read, bringing a less than stealthy grin to my face.

My heart swelled with anticipation.

Midnight couldn't come fast enough!

"Sloane!" Susan called from the poolside. "What's that in your hands?"

I almost dropped the letter but crumpled it up and put it in the nearest garbage can before Susan could demand to read it. "Just a piece of trash," I responded, hoping that she believed me. "Trying to do my duty and clean up the stands."

Susan gave me an odd look before nodding her head. "Let's hit the showers. You should rest up a little tonight, go to bed early. You seemed a little distracted today during practice, and I saw that you were talking to Natalie Coughlin for a while."

So Susan *had* noticed. Oh no! I had to be careful. Jae Sung was getting to my head too much, and it was causing me to be distracted from my practice. But I couldn't stop meeting him or thinking about him – and I wouldn't. This was worth the cost…wasn't it?

All I could manage to say was a feeble apology to Susan.

"Don't apologize to me," she retorted, a smug look on her face. "You want the gold? You gotta focus more. Tomorrow is a new day, so it's a chance for you to start over."

That. *That's* what I loved about Susan – she was always willing to look on the bright side. In fact, when Mom and I were looking for a coach for me, the optimism that Susan had was one of the biggest perks to her. Well, that and the fact that she had won three gold medals in the Olympics before becoming a full-time Olympics swim coach.

"You're right," I agreed, joining her in the walk to the showers. "New start tomorrow."

As I let the hot water run down my hair and my body, my thoughts turned round and round about Jae Sung. Would it be possible to see him *and* do well at the Olympics? I couldn't let him go, so I guess I was going to find out.

But first, I needed to watch Jae Sung at *his* practice, which was scheduled right after mine. I wondered how he would do, what were his strengths when it came to his athleticism. It would be a *dream* to practice together, which would actually be odd since usually, the swimmers practice with people of their same gender. *That needed to change,* I thought.

After hitting the showers, I climbed the stands to watch some of the guys from the North Korean team (including Jae Sung) practice alongside the Italians, guys from Turkey and some Russian male swimmers. I spotted Jae Sung heading down, already unzipping his jacket. My eyes and heart *willed* him to look my way, but to no avail.

My heart sank when I didn't catch Jae Sung's attention, but I knew I would have the opportunity while he practiced. Obviously, he was focused on his own practice now, having seen mine.

As I settled back in the stands, I noticed a familiar person walking toward the stands: Grace! Her face was all smiles as she made a beeline for me and plopped down right next to me.

"Hey!" she chirped, her voice full of enthusiasm. "My practice finished early, and I figured I would come chill with you for a while!"

For a second, I was enthused at the possibility of hanging out with my new friend. Then, I was reminded that she knew nothing about me and Jae Sung. In fact, no one knew about my new relationship. If Jae Sung were any other guy from any other team and any other country, this wouldn't be a big deal. *Why couldn't he just have been from Australia or something?*

"Watching someone?" Grace's words broke into the fantasy in my mind.

"Hmm?" I asked distractedly, then literally shook my head to regather myself. "I mean, maybe. I just want to see how the guys do from other countries."

Wowwwww…great response, Sloane, I scolded myself, willing my face to remain in the current color it was and not turn beet red.

I soon discovered that my face could be any shade and Grace would recognize my thoughts immediately and pull them out from me. She must've been a mind reader or something.

"Mmmmhmmm," she replied, a mischievous grin appearing on her face. "You *are* watching someone! Tell me, does his home country feature the best pasta in the world or the famous baklava?"

This time, there was *no* controlling my face.

It broke out in an involuntary grin, and I turned to face my new friend. "Wouldn't you like to know?"

Grace sighed, turning away from me to look out at the water as Jae Sung and his fellow male athletes warmed up. She shrugged her shoulders nonchalantly and said, "Well, they're *all* hot, so that's all that matters."

"Yeah, that's all that matters," I agreed with a quick nod of my head. I settled back in the stands and turned toward the water, ready and eager to watch Jae Sung show his power.

CHAPTER TEN

Jae Sung (재성)

As I climbed up on the podium in front of the swimming pool, my heart started beating wildly in my chest. This was just *one* practice, but I had noticed that Sloane had stayed behind to watch.

This would be the first Gala where someone besides my family and my coach would be watching. Someone outside of my own ethnicity, my own country, would have eyes on me as I took to the water to warm up.

I had noticed Sloane as I got in place in front of the pool, but she was too engrossed with her friend to look at me. Would she even be willing to talk to me in public anyway? What if my minder, my team, or someone else saw? Would we get in trouble for talking to someone from another country, too?

Hastily, I reminded myself that I did not have time to think about such things. Every practice counted, and this one was no different. My feelings for Sloane would have to be put aside, for just this hour, as I showed my fellow North Koreans what I could do. *Proved* myself to them, more so.

Like always, I swung my arms back and forth, warming up my limbs, and did some squats on top of the podium too. I pulled my goggles down over my eyes and took position, readying my body and my mind for the first hit of the water on my face.

There would be no whistles to start my practice, as that was saved for the competition only. This was all me.

Eagerly, I took my first dive and started pumping my arms, my legs, my body, driving myself forward. The water met me, wrapping itself warmly around me, and I felt myself getting relaxed as I glided through the water. With each new stroke, I felt like myself again, for just a moment, the worries about the world around me fading away.

Curiously, I looked over to my right, noticing the guy from Italy gaining speed on me. This was not a competition, but I wanted Sloane to know that I was *the best* that North Korea had to offer. Maybe I was showing off a little…

I forced myself to go further, to dig deeper, to push harder, until my hand hit the wall. Then, I did my turn and made my way effortlessly back to the other side of the pool.

Just when I thought Mr. Italiana was keeping pace with me, I found (to my delight) that he had slacked off some. Unfortunately, so had my muscles. They burned and ached with overuse.

I could hear my coach's and my minder's voices in my mind: *Remember your practices are for just that – practice. They are not to show who is the best swimmer!*

Relinquishing my ego, I let my mind and my body go into a familiar rhythm, sinking into an easygoing pace. My body thanked me as the pain in my legs and arms subsided.

When I reached the end of the pool, I gripped the wall and bobbed up and down in the water, searching for the place I had seen Sloane sit down. Instead of talking with Grace, she was now staring directly at me. So was Grace.

Carelessly, I shared a small smile with her, then turned my attention back to the pool.

Who cares if anyone sees me? I thought rebelliously. *It was just one smile.*

At that moment, I felt free. Not just because I was swimming, but because I could share my feelings with someone who was beginning to know me so well.

"Hey, North Korea!" a guy who was clearly from South Korea yelled in Korean to me.

Though we were from two different countries, we shared the same blood inside of us. Our language was similar, too, so I could understand almost one hundred percent of what my South Korean peers were saying. I tested this theory when I was standing in line for signing in on the first day of my arrival in China.

My mind flashbacked to that day. We were tired from our long trip to get to Beijing, and all I wanted to do was get to our room and sleep, but my coach let me and my team know that we would have to sign in before getting our keys to our rooms in the Olympic Village. Oddly enough, the South Korean swimming team happened to be in front of us in line.

Their white team outfits blazed bright like headlights and their hair was tamed by massive amounts of gel. I quickly noted how their bodies were a little thicker than ours as well. Also, most of the South Koreans were taller than us North Koreans, I realized. Both the height and weight indicated to me that they must be able to eat more.

As I stood behind one guy who was about four inches taller than me, they joked back and forth about the different girls they wanted to get to know from various countries.

I tuned into their conversation and found that I did not miss a word.

Today was no different. Even though it was only a few words that the South Korean swimmer had yelled at me, I understood them all.

"Hey, are you deaf, North Korea?" he teased me, bobbing in time with me in the water, his body full facing mine.

"What do you want?" I replied, annoyed that my practice was stopped by this guy. It could have been any other country and I would have been okay.

"What do you think, being outside of your country? It must be a complete shock for you. I heard they keep you guys locked up in chains all day."

My stomach soured at his rude and degrading remarks. This guy was talking about something he did not even know anything about. *No one* is allowed into North Korea without permission, South Koreans included. My grandmother often told me that outsiders had snuck into our country (mostly by crossing the river illegally) and that their fate was not a good one.

Death, torture, imprisonment, government bribery to get their citizens back. There was never a good outcome. This guy would not last five seconds in my country, I was sure of it.

"I heard that you guys in South Korea will suck someone's dick for five dollars. Anything for the money," I responded, a smile playing on my lips.

I gave myself the satisfaction of seeing my South Korean counterpart's mouth drop open in shock, then I turned back to the task at hand.

Practice.

If I had to race this guy, I promised myself I would do everything in my power to beat him.

CHAPTER ELEVEN

Sloane

After Jae Sung's practice, I joined Grace in the cafeteria at the Olympic Village. We both got some salads with eggs on top (for protein) then made our way to a table near the window.

It was surprisingly a bright day in Beijing today, the sun beaming down on us fervently. Since my team and I had arrived in this city, the sky was covered by gray. The sun was a nice change and reminded me of back home.

"Have you been able to see the city yet?" Grace asked me, gingerly pouring some Italian dressing on her salad before taking a big bite of lettuce and tomatoes.

"No, not yet. I need to, though. When do we find the time?"

Grace informed me that her coach had given them a full day to wander the city. I wish that was the case for me. Susan was on my tail 24/7. It would be so nice to have a day to explore this city, especially since it was my first time in another country.

What would be even nicer was sightseeing with Jae Sung. That was just an irrational dream, though, I knew.

"So, let's get to the topic at hand, shall we?" Grace wiggled her eyebrows up and down in a flirty manner.

I knew she would want to talk about Jae Sung. She must've seen the smile we shared. Here we go…

"Who was that guy in the pool that you smiled at? Spill the tea! Have you guys been able to talk yet?" Grace rambled on in what sounded like one sentence without taking a breath.

"Hold your horses or you might choke on your salad, my friend," I retorted, sipping my lemonade like I had all the time in the world. "He's just someone I noticed in the pool and he looks nice."

Grace shook her head slowly from side to side. "Sloane, you are *not* good at lying. So what does Susan think about it?"

I continued to downplay my interaction with Jae Sung, worried about what she would think.

Would we get in trouble for talking? Would I get *him* in trouble?

"Really, he's no one to me. Just some hot swimmer," I promised, the lie burning its way down my throat and causing tears that I tried to hide.

Grace didn't believe me for one second, but she chose to lay the matter down. For now anyway. We returned to our lunch and chatted about our families, school, and hometowns. Anything but the cute North Korean who shared a smile with me.

Later that night, as I climbed the steps, I thought about whether or not I should warn Jae Sung that Grace was on to it. As I swung the rooftop doors open, I decided against it.

The night hadn't changed from the last two nights – but it was substantially cooler tonight for some reason. I wrapped my arms around my arms, which were ladled with new goosebumps.

Jae Sung sat casually on the couch, our couch, his legs tucked under him. He looked peaceful at that moment, looking out at the city.

I cleared my throat to let my new boyfriend know I had arrived and he turned toward me, all smiles from ear to ear.

"It was so good to watch you practice today!" Jae Sung let me know, hurrying toward me and pulling my body close to his.

I inhaled his now familiar smell: sandalwood, or some earthy scent. I buried my face into his shoulder, not letting go of his frame as my arms wrapped around him.

"Likewise," I countered, leaning back to look into his murky brown eyes. "You did really well today!"

No more talking. Jae Sung put his hands to my face and brought my lips to his without another moment's hesitation. Our mouths collided hungrily and our tongues tangoed back and forth, sending shivers down my spine.

This guy was so amazing. Where would I find another male like him? Probably nowhere.

"Grace knows about me, no?" Jae Sung inquired, flopping down beside me on the haggard couch.

I shook my head adamantly. "No way. She asked over lunch today, but I downplayed it."

A look of relief washed over Jae Sung's face. "Good. I do not know yet what my coach or my minder would think."

How long could we hide in plain sight? If Grace had caught our exchange, it was only a matter of time before Jae Sung's babysitter caught on.

What would that mean for him?

"We have to be more careful next time. All I want to do is look at you, but it could get you into some serious trouble," I whispered to Jae Sung, twining my fingers through his.

"I think I am okay to risk it all for you," he promised me, leaning over to plant a sweet, small kiss on my lips. "You are changing my heart."

I wrapped my arms once more around his torso, willing my body to join with his as I slid into his lap. Gone was the *good girl Sloane*, replaced with this mad woman who would do *anything* to be close to this former stranger.

Breaking the kiss, Jae Sung mentioned to me that there was an encounter with a guy from the South Korean swim team while he was in the pool.

"I think I read in the news that South and North Korea don't like talking, right?" I wondered.

He confirmed my suspicions with a nod. "It is unfortunate, but since the Fatherland Liberation War –"

"What is *that?* Is it the Korean War?" I interrupted, curiosity tugging at every part of me.

Jae Sung didn't seem to mind that I had interrupted him. "Yes, it is loosely called that in our country, but mostly, we call it the Fatherland Liberation War."

Interesting. Everything had its own thing in North Korea.

"Even though our citizens do not talk, this guy communicated with me, and I can understand every word they speak. Our languages are very similar, except for what you call, *slang?*"

Ah. So they *did* understand each other. Was that a good or bad thing?

"Is it illegal for South Koreans to go into North Korea?" I asked Jae Sung, leaning toward him in anticipation of his answer.

"Yes, unfortunately so. Anyone who tries to come into my country without a permit may be shot on sight. South Koreans will immediately be put into prison camps, killed, or used as a leveraging bargain between the South and the North."

This was so insane! And here I was, kissing this guy on top of a rooftop in Beijing like it was something kosher. But I couldn't deny my heart the way it felt. I *had* to be with him. He couldn't help where he was born anymore than I could.

We sat there for the next few hours, me asking random questions about North Korea, and Jae Sung answering them all without a moment's hesitation. I could've sat with him until the sun came up, but we both had to get back to our rooms so we could get at least a *few* hours of shut eye.

As we walked toward the rooftop door, hand-in-hand, I stopped and turned toward Jae Sung. "Promise me one thing. When we leave, you and I will still talk."

"If we can do more than that, I would be happy. I want to be with you, Sloane," Jae Sung admitted, his thumb playing absentmindedly with mine.

"I want to be with you too," I affirmed, leaning into him to give him one last kiss before we both went down the stairwell at different times.

But at what cost?

CHAPTER TWELVE

Jae Sung (재성)

Sun filtered in through the thin brown curtains of the window of my room that I shared with four other North Korean swimmers. It was the morning after our last meeting, and I had dreamt about her. Sloane. The girl who had captured my heart and mind.

In the dream, we were on a plane traveling to America, our hands clasped together on the seat rest in-between us. *Wishful thinking.*

Was that a dream, or was it real? I knew that I wanted to be with her, even after the first meeting with her. Would that mean me leaving my home country, my parents? What would I do to be with her?

I was only eighteen years old, and in two weeks, I would be attending the prestigious Kim Il Sung University, named after our Founding Father Kim Il Sung. My grades at Ansan High School were very good, and I knew that I could get a scholarship to the Supreme Leader's college. Was that what *I* wanted though?

Fear shot through my veins like ice. All of my life, I had been told what I should do by my parents, by my government, my abeoji and my abba, my eomma, another voice in the equation. What about what *I* desired? Did that matter?

There were so many places to go, so many countries to see, so many various universities that I could attend. Why did I have to stay in my home country to go to school? Even though we had been told that North Korea was a mecca for us, was it really? I was seeing the joy that the Westerners had, even those from Eastern countries like Japan and Thailand. What about us North Koreans? We had known oppression and control from those who ruled our land.

I shook these rebellious thoughts from my head at once. One night with an American girl, and I was already feeling oppositional toward the people who fed me, who cared for me, and clothed me.

What was wrong with me? Was it her fault, or was it mine?

My thoughts swam a little further around in my mind until my minder, Byung Hun, touched my shoulder, shaking me as if to awaken me from a deep sleep, though my eyes were open.

"Jae Sung," he spoke my name gently but with a bit of authority in his voice, "*Il-eonaseo bab-eul meoggo yeonseubhaleo gaja.*" ("Get up, let us eat, and let us get going to your practice.")

A glance around the room showed me that the rest of my teammates were busy eating already, the steam from their bowls of rice flowing through the sunshine peeking into our room.

Had I slept in? That would not be good! I was here for one job and one job only – to make the Supreme Leader proud by winning a gold medal for my country's glory!

Hastily, I popped up in my bed, and Byung Hun handed me an already-steaming bowl of rice, which I consumed quicker than I should have, excited to get to the pool.

When we arrived at the practice pool, our lanes were empty ghosts, waiting for us to fill them with our bodies. Disappointment coursed through me when I realized that Sloane was not in the stands, like I had been for her.

Of course not, Jae Sung. It is only five a.m. Our team chose the earliest time slot for practice so that we would look like we were as serious about our practices as we are about our game days, I silently reminded myself.

Stepping out of my white trainers, my blue and red North Korean hoodie and sweatpants, I slipped on my swim cap, tucking my hair neatly underneath it. Shaking my arms outward and side to side, I took the time to warm up before dipping a toe into the pool. My ritual was to dip my toe "for good luck." It was something I had been doing since I was a little boy, according to my eomma. Do not ask me why.

Eagerly, I slipped the rest of my body into the pool, the water suctioning to my skin in its old familiar way like a glove on the hand.

My mind drifted back to my Olympic tryouts back in Pyongyang. There were only three-hundred North Korean men and boys chosen from the age of fifteen to thirty (no older, no younger) to try out for the swim team. Our Supreme Leader wanted us fit and young, the best of the best. It was such an honor to even be chosen for tryouts! Perhaps the Supreme Leader had seen me at my high school swim practices, I remember thinking foolishly and wishfully.

I performed my tryout like I was on autopilot, a machine programmed to do its very best by my own abeoji, a man skilled at perfectionistic behavior and attitudes. My tryout went so well, in fact, that I was in the top three for my age group – number two, to be exact.

Our team did not ride in a plane to get to China. Instead, we crossed over the border between North Korea and China. Anyone who crosses over the border between China and North Korea without official papers will be shot, arrested, or put in a concentration camp immediately, but our team had papers straight from the Supreme Leader himself. I can remember seeing the surprised look on the border guard's face as he read the official document from Kim Il Jung.

"*Gim-Iljung-ui myeonglyeong-e ttala i salamdeul-eul jinagage haeya handa. geudeul-eun 2008nyeon jung-gug beijing ollimpig-eseo widaehan bughan-in uli jogug-eul wihae gong-yeonhal yejeong-ida,*" the letter read. ("By order of Kim Il Jung, you must let these people pass. They will be performing for our country, the great nation of North Korea, in the 2008 Olympics in Beijing, China.")

"*Igeo sagiya?*" the border guard questioned, a look of incredulous disbelief sprayed across his worn-out face. *Is this a joke?*

Byung Hun immediately spoke up, relaying that this was not a farce, and the guard could contact the Supreme Leader if he felt that it was.

Thankfully, we made it through the border, and we drove in our three government-issued vans for two days straight to Beijing, stopping only for the restroom and food. Our minders drove the vans the whole time, and we kept them awake by talking about the great things about our land when Kim Il Sung was alive.

I did not get to know any of my teammates on that trip, though many of them talked amongst themselves like they were old best friends. My mind was set on one thing and one thing only: Winning the gilded badge at the Olympics.

Now. Now, my mind was on two things: Winning the gold of the games and gaining the golden opportunity of getting to know Sloane better. It was an awkward place for me to be in my heart and mind – I felt like I was two people inside one body.

As I finished my practice an hour later, I noticed that a few of the other swimming teams were making their way into the pool area, studying us with curious eyes. One of the teams was the American team, and when I saw Sloane, I felt my heart leap in my chest.

She did not notice me, though, because she was engaged in conversation with an older woman with red hair in a Team USA jersey. This woman looked protective over her.

Her coach, I assured myself as I pulled myself out of the pool, wrapping my already chilled body in a warm, thick towel.

We did not have towels like these back home. I relished in the comfort I got from this towel as I dried myself off. Maybe I could take one home, if just to give it to my eomma. She would love the feel of its luxury on her skin.

As I headed to the showers, I could not get there fast enough. I wanted to hurry to the stands so that I could watch Sloane practice.

"Eotteohge jinhaengdoego issnayo?" a member of my team, Ji Hoon, asked me as he turned on the faucet next to mine. "How is it going?"

"Johda!" I responded enthusiastically, turning to let the water hit my face and wet my hair. *"It's good!"*

"Have you seen the American swimmers? Hot piece of ass." Ji Hoon threw me a mischievous smile.

Something defensive rose up in me.

Jealousy? Was he talking about Sloane?

"You should be careful talking like that. Byung Hun might hear you and you could get into trouble," I reminded Ji Hoon, lathering up my body with soap.

Ji Hoon literally laughed out loud. "*Jja Jeung Na!* (Oh my god!) You sound like a parrot for the Supreme Leader."

I gave Ji Hoon an angry look. "Just be careful," I repeated, then turned off the water with a huff.

As I retreated to the lockers to dress in my Team North Korea outfit, I heard Ji Hoon whisper to himself in disdain, "I *namja* (this guy)." I just chose to let it go. He was the least of my worries…but I reminded myself to watch out for him. I did not want to be pulled into his trouble or to even talk about women in the manner that he did.

Watching Sloane swim was like watching a goddess touch the earth. Her body looked perfect in the water, like she was made for it.

Eventually, she spotted me and we exchanged a smile. This was enough to make me feel much better after my angry interaction with Ji Hoon.

Pulling the pen and paper I had hidden out of my jacket, I scribbled a quick declaration for Sloane to read. I looked over at Byung Hun, who was too engrossed in a conversation with our team's swim coach to notice what I was doing.

Looking back at Sloane, I nodded downward and dropped the letter on the floor. She nodded back, indicating she had seen it.

This could really work!

"Let us go back to the dorms for a while," Byung Hun advised the team and myself.

Not wanting to leave the stands, I still knew I had to follow orders. Reluctantly, I got up and followed everyone down the stairs.

I wish it was midnight already, I pondered, hope churning in my heart. Midnight could not come soon enough.

CHAPTER THIRTEEN

Sloane

This time, it was *me* waiting for Jae Sung on the rooftop of our building. When he arrived, I had my legs slung over the couch, and I was texting my parents about my practices. *How is it going? Do you feel ready?* I could feel their worry seep into me all the way across the Pacific Ocean.

I reassured Mom and Dad that my practices were going well. No, I didn't tell them about Jae Sung. It would only make them both upset, to know that I was "wasting my time with a guy instead of having my head in the right place."

When the door to the rooftop opened, I practically ran into Jae Sung's arms. We shared a warm, tight hug before making our way back to the couch.

"Thanks for your note," I told him as we sat down comfortably together, legs touching once more.

"You're welcome. You looked so good out there – strong. Are you ready for tomorrow?"

Shrugging, I studied my hands with creeping anxiety mounting in me. "Not really. I can't believe that all of my training has come to *this*. The day is finally here!"

Jae Sung agreed with me by nodding, his mild brown eyes trained on my face. "I feel as ready as I can be. However, I cannot stop thinking of you. In fact, I had a dream about you last night. We were going to America together."

My face immediately painted blush red and I couldn't stop it. What would a future with Jae Sung look like? Would we live together, go to college at the same school, and would he be able to leave North Korea?

"What's it like in North Korea?" I found myself asking, the words tumbling out of my mouth without the ability to stop them.

Jae Sung slung an arm around my shoulders and I leaned into him. "I do not know what it is like in America, but in my country, we cannot travel outside of our city or outside of North Korea without approval. I had to get approval to come to the Olympics. A group of us came to the games in vans with a pass from our Supreme Leader."

My eyes involuntarily widened. I couldn't *imagine* not being able to travel without permission from the government. Yes, permission from my parents, since I was still underage – but asking for President Obama to let me go somewhere? Out of the question. What must a life like that feel like, so trapped?

"Do you like living there? Is it where you want to live for the rest of your life?" I grabbed Jae Sung's hand in mine, squeezing it to show my affection.

Jae Sung adamantly shook his head, his raven-black hair falling over his face as he did. "Please keep this between you and me, but I would like to leave North Korea. Also, I would like to get my parents out. My abeoji – my grandfather – loves our nation, of course, but my parents, my sister, and I all have our objections to the way things are run. Of course, we cannot voice these in public, for it would mean death or imprisonment."

Obviously, I hadn't done my research on North Korea. These stark facts hit me like a freight train going ninety miles an hour. I was dizzy with shock to my soul. *Not being able to question your government without fear of punishment?* What kind of world would that be? I wouldn't survive there, without a doubt; in fact, I would probably be in prison the moment my mouth opened.

My grandmother, Lolly, was a hardcore protester. She protested the Vietnam War, protested in the 1960's for civil rights, and made her position known by voicing support for LGBTQ rights. You would be right if you bet that I got my fighting spirit from her!

"I wonder how you can get out of North Korea," I pondered.

These were all sexy things to be talking about, of course. I had never been one to engage in a conversation that wasn't deep. Maybe that's why I didn't mesh well with the guys at my school. Most of them were just too immature for me. Now Jae Sung – he was able to hold a levelheaded conversation, and he didn't seem interested in just locking lips with me. I liked that.

"Tell me about you," Jae Sung requested, dipping his head close to mine. I thought for a moment that he would kiss me, but his face just stayed there, peering at me with utmost curiosity.

I told Jae Sung about life in Cape Cod – how my family and I would visit the beach and stay in our beach house in the summers, how we would brace ourselves for the cold winters. I told him about our trips to the South to visit my uncle and aunt in Florida, where the weather was warmer year-round. We talked about high school life, and I discussed how I wanted to go to college abroad, but my mother would like me to go to a school close to our home.

Would I be able to go to school in China and could Jae Sung join me? That would be such a wonderful thing!

"May I kiss you?" Jae Sung interrupted my verbal thoughts, his eyes trained steadily on mine.

Never in my eighteen years had a guy *asked* to kiss me. They had just done it. This was a fresh, surprising gesture – and I loved it.

I could only nod my head as excitement pulsed through me from top to bottom, wetting my lips to get them ready for him.

Jae Sung dipped his head lower until his mouth met mine. He slowly worked his lips over mine, then cupped my head in his hands. When his tongue met mine, I gasped softly, a thrill running through my whole being.

The kiss deepened and I fell further into his arms, snuggling up to him until my legs were crossing his. I wrapped my arms around him too and pulled him even closer to me, not wanting to let go.

Suddenly, there was a loud *bang*, and Jae Sung and I flew apart from each other to opposite ends of the couch. What was that?!

Chloe strutted out onto the rooftop; a smug look was splayed across her face. She wore pink striped pajamas, her feet shoved into some furry white slippers.

"Chloe! What are you doing up here?"

"I woke up and saw you leaving our room and I was curious as to *where* you were going at *midnight.*"

Her emerald green eyes shone with anger. I met her gaze with an equal look of boldness, not backing down, but I didn't get up from my place next to Jae Sung. Instead, I waited for Chloe to say something else.

"I cannot believe you!" she shouted, ignoring my question, and I cringed at the sound of her voice like a kid being reprimanded by a parent. "We are at the Olympics and you're up here, smooching some random guy! What would Susan say?"

Oh no. Susan. Chloe and I shared the same swim coach, which was a fact I had forgotten. Of course, this girl would love nothing but to tell Susan about me. She would enjoy having our coach all to herself and snatching the gold for best freestyle swim time out from under me.

Inadvertently, I stole a glance at Jae Sung.

He didn't appear to be cowering in his corner of the couch, but he didn't look happy either. In fact, he wore a sickened look on his face. Would this get him into trouble, if he was found with me?

"Really, I don't think that's any of your business," I replied confidently, returning the self-righteous look that Chloe initiated. "What we do outside of practice and competitions is entirely our choice."

Chloe snorted, tossing her messy red hair over her shoulder in what must be her signature move. "Tell Susan that. See what she says," she challenged me with a sneer.

I got up and stood right in front of her. "You tell Susan about this, and you will completely regret it," I threatened Chloe, matching her challenge with an equal look of disdain.

"Oh yeah? What're you gonna do?" Chloe arched an eyebrow.

My mind raced. What *could* I do? Pushing Chloe off the roof would certainly get me disqualified from the games, if not more. My only option would *have* to be to tell Susan, before Chloe did.

"I'll tell Susan tomorrow," I offered, rearranging my face into a triumphant stare as I bore my eyes into Chloe's green ones.

That seemed to suffice, for Chloe blew out a breath and shrunk back a little like the mangy dog she was, looking for scraps from me. "Just watch your back. You think you can beat me for the gold, but you're wrong."

So *that* was why Chloe was tormenting me – she was afraid I would beat her! "I care more about this guy than I do the gold. I'm going to go out there and do my best, but he is what matters now." Wow. I realized immediately that those words were one hundred percent true.

Chloe shook her head with disbelief. "You practiced and practiced, then you come here and you're so ready to win until you meet *him?* He's a North Korean – it's not like he can go anywhere with you after the games are over."

Her words hit me with a bucket of truth like a tornado bearing down on my house. Jae Sung would most likely *not* be able to follow me to America after the Olympics. Were we just playing with fire here, engaging in something that wouldn't pan out? Or was there more to the story – would he be able to leave North Korea?

I didn't know the answer to those questions, but I *did* know that my time with him *now* was precious to me...and it was being wasted on Chloe.

Jae Sung sat still, not uttering a word. I didn't need him to defend me, but it surprised me how quiet he was. Was it uncommon for North Korean guys to talk to girls? If so, why or how was he able to muster up the courage to talk to me? Was he just shy?

"*This* matters now. Just mind your business and focus on your swimming," I advised Chloe, turning my back on her and returning to sit on the couch.

With a shrug of her shoulders, Chloe's voice took on a challenging tone. "That makes more room for me to win the gold I came here for."

This girl. I never understood females like her that needed to challenge others to feel good about themselves. Just be you, don't worry about what others think. Do your best for *yourself*. *You* are your only competitor.

I didn't reply to Chloe because that would give her too much satisfaction. Instead, I turned my attention back to Jae Sung and stared at him until our gazes turned into smiles stretched across our faces.

Chloe gave up with a sigh and went back into the stairwell, closing the door behind her. *Good riddance, witch.*

"That was intense," Jae Sung commented, his face taut with worry. "Will you get in trouble?"

"Nah," I shook my head, trying to convince myself more than anyone else. "I'll let my coach know tomorrow. No biggie. She's *my coach*, not my mom and dad."

"What will your mom and dad say though?" Jae Sung wondered, running his hand through my hair gently.

"My mom wants this more than my dad, maybe more than me. In college, my mom was a swimmer. She actually went out for the Olympics, but she didn't make it. That's why her dream is for me to score a medal." My heart sank with the accuracy of my statement.

Jae Sung let out a breath of frustration. "Aaaaaish," he muttered. I wondered what that meant but recognized it as a sound of frustration almost immediately. "My parents are so proud of me for getting this far. I must make the Supreme Leader proud too. This could ruin my future. I want to be with you, but I do not want to disappoint my family and my country."

Wow. So this was the end? I could see my relationship with Jae Sung continuing after the games, but I guess not anymore.

"Also, if my minder catches me, I could be sent to prison or killed when I return to North Korea," Jae Sung added, fear rising in his eyes and his voice.

I couldn't even imagine being killed or in prison because of someone you loved. Love? Was that what this was? I had never been in love before. Sure, I had *read* a lot of books about love – books from the romance section of Barnes and Noble. This could be love...I couldn't stop thinking about Jae Sung, and I didn't want to.

"Do you want to stop meeting?" I asked, surprised that it was only the third time we had met yet it might be the last.

Jae Sung didn't speak for a while. He looked far off into the city beyond the rooftop, his gaze taking on one that looked like he was sleepwalking.

"I do not *want* to stop. But we may *have* to.

If we get found out –"

I took his hands in mine before he could continue that statement. "Chloe is just lying," I reassured Jae Sung. "There's no way she would tell anyone. She's threatened by me, that's all. Maybe I can give her my spot so she will stop bothering us."

"Give up your chance for a medal? No!" Jae Sung thundered back, and I jolted on the couch.

"You must try your best! Do not give up."

We sat like that for a moment, both lost in our own thoughts.

"Let us continue to meet," Jae Sung decided. "Please. I cannot bear the thought of not meeting you."

I leaned forward to peck his cheeks with my lips eagerly. He turned his head so that his lips met mine once more, and we were locked in a heavier kiss than the first. My hands ran through Jae Sung's hair energetically, relishing in how he felt so close to me.

I didn't want this to end...no way. Yet I didn't want Jae Sung to get into deep trouble that could get him killed or captured. What would we do?

CHAPTER FOURTEEN

Jae Sung (재성)
One Week Ago

The lights went out in my home, signaling that it was time for "lights out" in the city. I peered out my window to confirm that it was okay for me to pull out my illegal laptop, and I was thrilled to find that it was safe to do so.

Laying down on my stomach on my *yo* on the floor, I pulled my laptop out from under the mat. It was not a very good hiding place, but sans cutting a hole in the wall or the floor, it was the only place that I had to keep my contraband hidden.

One thing that had never occurred to me was the fact that the North Korean government could track what I was searching. Nothing had come up as I had used the laptop repeatedly on previous occasions, so I had no cause for alarm.

Eagerly, I typed "Beijing" into the search engine, desperate to find out more about the first city outside of my country that I would be visiting. A message came up in bold, white letters, surrounded by a red square that filled my screen. "*Igeos-eul*

geomsaeghal su eobs-seubnida. daleun geomsaeg-eul sidohasibsio."
("You cannot search for this. Please try another search.")

My heart immediately raced in my chest, threatening to jump out of me, and I felt a lump form in my throat. Fears of being arrested or killed raced through my head.

Would the People's Security come arrest me now, taking me to a labor camp and killing or arresting my family as well? Would I be killed in a public execution in the town's city center for all to see (which was so common in our country)?

I waited a moment, the seconds seeming like hours as I anticipated my fears coming to pass.

Nothing happened, though, and no other messages appeared on my screen.

Let's try searching for some South Korean music, I decided, typing into the search engine.

Surprisingly, no message came up, and I was able to see pictures of men and women dressed in chic clothing pop up on my screen. The men had semi-long hair, which was highly uncommon on the men in North Korea. Most men (including myself) opted for short-cropped hair.

Their faces were shiny, poised, and they actually looked happy.

Eagerly, I clicked the first picture I found. It took me to a site called YouTube, which was evidently a video site. I was shocked to find it was not blocked as well.

A song immediately started playing so loud on my screen and I rushed to turn it down. "Listen boy…", some peppy girl band named Girls Generation belted out too fast for me to stop the video.

My *eomeoni* passed by my room at that moment, though, causing me to jump and shove the laptop under my mat. I knew she had seen it. Diving under my covers, I pretended to be asleep.

My eomeoni is wise, and she knows me well though. She peeked her head into the room with a grin on her beautiful face.

"Jae Sung, *dangsin-i jamdeulji anh-assdaneun geos-eul algo issseubnida.*" ("I know you are not asleep.")

Sheepishly, I turned toward her, keeping my eyes trained on the ground out of respect. "*Ne, Eomeo?*" I whispered, hoping my informal greeting would soften her heart toward me.

Surely she had seen the laptop. According to our government, it was each person's responsibility to report illegal activity to the People's Security, no matter if they were family or not. Would my own mother disclose my indiscretion?

"I saw the laptop," she replied to me in Korean, her voice hard and firm.

I knew right then that I was in trouble.

Thoughts of my eomeoni declaring my error to our police force flooded my brain, and my body immediately broke out in a cold sweat. I was sure to be killed or arrested now.

"Ne," was all I could respond with, not having any words to cover up my crime.

"You do know that we could be in trouble," my mother whispered, and that indicated to me that she did not want my father to hear. This was good news! I felt my heartbeat slow down, and the tension I did not know that I had held flood out of my body.

"Ne," I acknowledged with my head bowed so low that it almost touched the cold cement floor. I felt lower than cow dung at this moment. "*Mianhaeyo. Yongseohae juseyo.*" ("I'm sorry. Please forgive me.")

What a feeble response I gave my own mother! However, what else could I say? I was caught, there was no getting out of this, and I could not offer any explanation.

"Now that I know that you have it, scoot over. I would like to sit next to you and see what you were looking at," my mother informed me, approaching with a smile on her face.

Huh! My own mother wanted to use my prohibited gear! This would be interesting.

Newly unashamed, I pulled up the video again, not as surprised that it was not blocked this time. My mom and I bopped our heads along to the music of South Korea's own Girls Generation for a full thirty minutes before Mom took over to look up older South Korean music.

For the next few hours, my mother and I huddled under a blanket on my yo on the cold floor of our home in Pyongyang, our minds opening to a world we had never known before. We went on to listen to "Nobody" by another girl band named The Wonder Girls, "Haru Haru" by a boy band called Big Bang (who looked like bad asses, if I had to say so myself), and "10 out of 10" by a band called 2 PM.

No more red boxes with words of warning came up for some reason. Maybe it was the magic that my mother carried with her. She was a special woman with the power to work miracles on anyone and anything she encountered.

Still, seeing all of the music I was missing out on because my country required us to only listen to government-sanctioned music was disheartening. I wanted to be able to listen to this music on a regular basis, without being in fear of being in trouble. The teenagers in South Korea were so lucky and I could not help but feel jealous of them! If I had been born in South Korea, I would be able to listen to K-Pop (a phrase I learned that night) on a regular basis.

However, all of my curiosity about the world was shared with at least one member of my family, who was eager to learn just as much as I was and would not be telling on me. I was not alone.

CHAPTER FIFTEEN

Sloane
One Week Ago

He had a change of heart. I knew that my dad was at least okay with me pursuing my swimming goals when he offered to take me out for some shopping for new swimming caps. This man *never* went shopping with me or my mom, and he loathed the ritual so much that he hung out at the front of the store until we were finished.

Our first stop was a local swim shop called Everything But Water. They had supplied multiple swimming singlets for me in the past, as well as most of my swimming gear, so I knew I could find some really good swim caps there.

On the drive there, my dad was stoic, his eyes trained on the road like it was his last drive ever in his silver Lexus UX. His hands stayed at ten and two on the wheel, and he was obviously gripping hard because his knuckles were white.

I swallowed the lump in my throat and chose to break the silence. "How was the surgery today?"

There was never really anything to talk about with my dad except for his work. We didn't have much in common, much less than me and my mother. Plus, he was at work so much that I felt that *the hospital* was his home away from home.

"It went well. We operated on a sixty-five-year-old woman with lung cancer, and it was successful," he replied methodically, his voice even and low.

My mind raced at what to ask next or what to talk about. "Dad?" I turned in my seat to look at him, my eyes already pricking with tears at the corners.

"Yes?" he immediately replied, not turning toward me but staying focused on the road.

How could I ask if we were okay? In what way would I be able to phrase that I wanted him to accept me and love me as I was? We had never had a deep discussion so this was going to be difficult, but I wanted to get closer to my father. Also, I wanted him to know how I felt.

"Dad, I need to know that you love me, that you accept me for me, and that you support my plans. That is important to me." Wow. I said it. It was out there. I felt my whole body relax into the leather seats, and I blew out a breath that I didn't know I was holding.

My father was quiet for a beat, the expression on his impassive face unchanged. Then, letting out a deep sigh, he countered, "I will always love you and support you no matter what. Sloane, I'm sorry if I have been hard on you. You know that my childhood was hard for me so I have worked hard to provide everything for you that I never had."

Here we go again, the "poor me, I was a child in poverty" spiel. I turned my head to look out at the trees passing us by on the highway and rolled my eyes but immediately felt guilty for my reaction.

I need to put myself in his shoes, I admonished myself.

"Yes, I remember. Thank you for that."

My dad's face tranquilized a little, and a small smile even formed on his face. It was the first one I had seen while he was in my presence in a while, actually.

"I'm sorry if I have been hard on you. It comes from a place of love, I promise. Can you forgive me?"

Oh. My. Gosh! My dad had *never* uttered those words to me before! This was *definitely* a different kind of day between us!

"Of course," I turned in my seat to look at him again.

"From now on, I will support you no matter what. If you have any questions about anything whatsoever while you are away at school, I am all ears too," my dad responded, facing me for the first time during this whole awkward ride.

Something in my heart unfroze, and the resistance toward my dad that I had felt for so long melted away. It was a new day!

With perfect timing, we arrived at the swim store. Dad parked the SUV in a spot, and we both hopped out without another word.

As we approached the door, my dad opened it for me. "After you," he gestured with his hand.

"Thanks, Dad," I said, feeling exhilaration shoot through me.

Now. Now I could be anything and do anything I wanted. I could live my life.

CHAPTER SIXTEEN

Jae Sung (재성)
Today

As I settled into my bed after what was a devastating ending to a wonderful time with Sloane, my thoughts swirled around in my head.

Everything was going so well. Sloane and I had shared a kiss, we had held hands, we were exchanging stories about our lives. Then, that girl came in and ruined it all. What was wrong with her? Why did it matter to her *what* Sloane and I did?

Yes, I knew that this hateful girl wanted to be a better swimmer than Sloane – in fact, I could see it in the way she looked at my girl. Did Chloe really think that she could keep me and Sloane apart though?

Should we stay apart? Could I find it within myself to stop seeing her? I doubted that I could, actually.

My eyes inadvertently drifted over to my minder, Byung Hun, who was so deep in sleep that his loud snores filled the room. Thankfully, *he* hadn't woken up and found Sloane and I talking on the roof. That would be my end, if he had.

There were only three more days at the Olympics, then our group would be heading back to North Korea. It was a gold medal or imprisonment for me, and I could not afford to lose at my swim meet. My practices had gone pretty well, despite being highly double-minded between my sport and my new love.

Love? Was *that* what I was feeling? Within three days, I had fallen in love with a stranger. No, she was no longer a stranger to me. Even though we had so much to learn about each other, I felt like I knew her better than the leader of my country, whom we North Koreans avidly study about from the time we are very young.

All I knew was that I was willing to risk my life, my citizenship, my very breath to be with this girl from Massachusetts, a place I had never been before. This was something I had never been willing to do, so it *must* be love.

I decided right then that I would tell Sloane that I loved her tomorrow. What would she say? I did not know. What I knew was that it was important that she knew how I felt about her, especially if we had to stop meeting. I wanted her to know that I did not want to stop seeing her, and even after we left the Olympics, I would still love to see her. Time, the ocean, space, and miles could not keep me away from Sloane. No matter the cost, I would do everything in my power to continue to be in her life, if she would have me.

In my country and my culture, love is not talked about verbally very much. Parents do not tell their children that they love them out loud, and spouses are not seen telling one another that they love each other with words. Love is *shown*, instead. I could tell my eomma and abba loved me from the way that they let me and my sister Ji Hye eat the bigger portion of rice rations every night. Also, my parents showed each other affection by helping each other out in the kitchen. In North Korea, love equals actions.

What could I do to *show* Sloane that I loved her? If I could have, I would wear a T-shirt that said her name and TEAM USA in big, bold letters on it! That would be a stupid action though, for it would most likely get me in trouble with Byung Hun.

Were my letters enough? Was meeting Sloane on the roof a sufficient supplement for verbally sharing my feelings with her? That would have to do, until I could find an alternative method which was worthy and safe.

Or I could just be like the Americans in the film I watched on my illegal laptop did – in *Love, Actually*, the actors *said* I love you to each other. Out loud. That was a big risk for me, but it was one I was willing to take.

Turning on my side, I faced the pictures of my family posted to the wall. *If I were to get in trouble, they would get in trouble too,* I reminded myself scornfully. *What kind of system allows people to get in trouble for loving someone?*

I could feel the icy intellectual shadow of the Juche system of my home country that I had stood in for so long start to melt away right then and there. If this was what my country was about, I did not want any part of it. Instead, I wanted to be somewhere where I could be free to love, free to be me, free to exist as I am. I did not want a minder following me around anymore, either, not even at the Olympics.

It may be time to somehow get rid of Byung Hun, to escape him so that you can go somewhere else with Sloane, I surmised to myself.

When I was a kid, before my halemoni died, she would get on her knees and speak quietly out loud to a man named Jesus. One day when I was eight years old, I caught her doing just that, hidden in the cloak of a darkened room with no candle as it was lights out for the night.

"Halmeoni, why do you talk out loud on your knees in a dark room? Who are you talking to?" I asked her, my eyes wide with wonder. "Is the Supreme Leader hidden in this room?"

With a laugh, my halmeoni replied, "No my dear. I am praying to someone bigger than the Great Leader, Comrade Kim Il Sung. His name is Jesus and he is God over all."

Turning my head to the side, weighing my grandmother's words, I narrowed my eyes. I knew better to question my grandmother out loud, for she was my elder, but in my heart, I wondered who this Jesus was.

My grandmother never got to tell me more, for she died from pneumonia a week later. She had been sick for some time, but she could not receive the medicine, which was held for only soldiers and the government.

Before I drifted off to sleep, I said a silent prayer to whatever god was out there besides the Dear Leader that Chloe would leave Sloane and me alone, or that Sloane would have favor with Susan when and if she told her.

CHAPTER SEVENTEEN

Sloane
Today

Today is the day. The day I have been preparing for since basically all of my life. The day that my mom and Susan and everyone on my team are counting on me to get at least a bronze medal for. The day that I am aiming for a gold medal.

Our team got to the pool earlier than we had to, just so that we could be prepared. Natalie (the other freestyle swimmer) and I were escorted to the warm-up waiting room while the individual medley swimmers went up first.

As I was stretching my hamstrings, I noticed Grace heading in my direction. Straightening up, I met her with a hug. "Heyyyyy!"

"Hey friend," she greeted me with a hug back, her jet-black hair pulled back in a tight ponytail. "How's it going? Are you feeling ready?"

Everyone and their mom had asked me that question a million times this morning before this very moment. Susan, nosy Chloe, my teammates, my mom via text. Their incessant badgering was creating nervous energy within me.

"As ready as I'll ever be," I responded with a weak smile. "I have been off my game for a few days, so I'm just shooting for a bronze at least."

Grace's coffee-brown eyes widened with surprise. "Sloane, you are better than that! You aren't a bronze level swimmer – you're a *gold* level swimmer! I believe in you!"

Her confidence boosted my spirit a little, and I felt my nerves melting away. "Thanks so much, Grace. I needed to hear that today."

Should I tell my friend about Jae Sung? If I were back home and I had met a guy, I would definitely tell my friends there. So yes, I should.

"I met a guy," I almost whispered, leaning toward Grace like the action of a teenage girl meeting a guy was a sin.

Grace's mouth gaped open, her pink-painted lips forming a perfect O. "Oh! My! Gosh!" she enunciated every word. "Do tell!"

We sat down in unison on one of the hard, metal benches. I took this time to continue to do stretches, even while sitting down because I would be going to the pool for my first competition soon.

"We saw each other at the Opening Ceremony and he invited me to join him on the rooftop of our dorm every night at midnight," I started, keeping my voice low so as not to allow anyone else to join our private conversation. "For the past few nights, we have been meeting."

"That's soooo romantic!" Grace rolled her eyes in time with her words. "Have y'all kissed yet? Where's he from? What's he look like?"

This was my chance to tell someone that Jae Sung was from North Korea. I braced myself for Grace's stunned response.

"Yes, we have kissed. FYI, it was AMAZING! As for looks, he's definitely hot. And – he's a swimmer too, so that is even better!" I began with the usual information. The last part was where I dipped my voice down into as low an octave as it would go. "He's from North Korea."

Grace literally jolted in the place where she was sitting. That told me all I needed to know for how Susan would react. I glanced around and caught Chloe staring at me as she stretched.

Surprisingly, her face broke into a grin — but it wasn't one of contempt or jealousy or anger. It was a genuine smile. Interesting...

"I don't know what to say," Grace admitted, rubbing her chin with her red, white, and blue manicured fingers. "How do you think your coach and your parents will respond if they find out?"

That question hit my heart tenfold. I felt myself dipping into a sort of depressive state. To be honest, I dreaded letting Susan and my mom and dad know, but I knew I had to do it. *Why* did it matter where someone was from? *Why couldn't* we just all drop the judgment and pretenses and just accept a person as they were, no matter *what?*

Shrugging my shoulders, I stood to stretch a little more. My competition time was just around the corner so I had to hurry. "I don't know. All I know is that I have to tell them because...I think I love him."

Grace gasped, covering her mouth with her hand. "Wellll, I *am* so happy for you and I will support you no matter what! So *that's* why you're worried about your swim time today! I would be worried too. But you know what? You got this girl! Don't fret — you were made for the gold!"

I high-fived my best friend just as Chloe came up. "May I talk to Sloane please?"

Grace narrowed her eyes at Chloe, the mutual dislike written all over her face. "Sure, but let me know if you need backup,

Sloane," she offered, walking back to the door that led to the stands.

Folding my arms over my chest, I locked my eyes on Chloe's. "What do you *want now*, Chloe?"

She let her arms drop to her sides in a neutral stance and her face showed one of remorse. "I'm so sorry about my behavior. To be honest, I was jealous of you. Am. I know you will at least medal up today. You're right – it's not my business what you do. So, I won't be telling Susan today."

My mouth fell open in amazement. "What brought on this sudden change of heart?"

Chloe shrugged. "I've just been thinking of this all night long. I realized that if I met a guy here, I would want my privacy with him, especially if he was from North Korea."

That last statement hit me hard. Everyone kept adding in where Jae Sung was from. Evidently, it was a bigger thing than I thought. Not to me, of course, but to everyone else.

"Well, thank you," was all I could mumble before an announcement came on over the loudspeaker.

"Will all freestyle swimmers please make their way to the poolside? Again, all freestyle swimmers, please make your way to the poolside." The message repeated in about five different languages other than English.

Susan took this time to come over to us, her conversation with an Olympics coordinator broken. Her face was one of earnest concern.

"Remember your training," she reminded both Chloe and me. "When you start to panic – because you will since that's normal – try to focus back on what your goal is. You can do this, girls!"

We both high-fived our coach before walking through the tunnel from the locker rooms to the poolside. My heart felt like it was going to beat out of my chest! This was it. Would I get gold?

Without a second thought, I glanced up into the stands and my eyes immediately found Jae Sung's face. I did a shy wave, my hand tucked near my chest. He returned the wave between his legs and near his feet so as not to alert his minder.

However, his minder happened to be looking at him at that moment. *Oh no!*

I noticed the stormy look in Byung Hun's eyes and the way he leaned over to tell Jae Sung something. Then, much to my horror, the two of them walked down the stairs and out the exit door, Jae Sung slinging me a look of desperation before he exited the room. *Oh my gosh! I hope he isn't in too much trouble!*

"Sloane," Chloe whispered to me, breaking my gaze and my chain of thought. "It's almost time. Get ready."

I noticed Chloe had already stripped down to her swimsuit and had put on her goggles and cap, so I did the same. Would Jae Sung miss my competition? More importantly, would he have to leave the Olympics? What was going to happen to him?

As I stepped onto the diving board, I glanced around at the other competitors. Chloe and I are from the USA. Swimmers from China, the Netherlands, Australia, and India were competing against us today, in this first heat.

Essentially, Chloe was my competitor in this heat, though we were both from the USA. I was trying to take gold from her as well as the other girls I was swimming against.

With a couple more shake outs of my arms, I bent down and prepared myself to dive into the crystal blue waters that were so familiar to me.

Before the foghorn went off, I stole a glance at the stands and noticed Jae Sung come running back into the room and up the stands, his minder following close behind him. It looked like his minder wanted to say more to him, but he didn't, possibly because they were in public now, and Jae Sung sat further away from him this time.

While I was glad he was here to see me compete, I was so worried about him. I couldn't wait for midnight to talk to him about what had happened with him and Byung Sun.

There was no more time to think about the trouble, though, because the foghorn went off. I dove into the water and began my first Olympic swimming competition.

CHAPTER EIGHTEEN

Jae Sung (재성)

This was my new girlfriend's big day. At least, that's what I thought she was. It was a slang that I had heard that Americans use, and I intended to use it too. Why? The feeling of joy filled my heart at the thought of Sloane being my "girl friend," a girl who was more than just a friend. My first *official* one, at that.

My fellow swimmers and I filed into the stands with Byung Hun at the tail end of our line. As this was not our time to swim, we arrived a little earlier than our competition hour began just to see the other swimmers. For some, it may have made them afraid to see the power they may be up against. However, for me, it gave me a sense of direction and focus – my mind became sharper by honing in on the skills of others with the same gift of swimming as myself.

Searching the pool diligently for Sloane, I could not find her. Immediately, I felt my heart grip with fear in my chest. Was she okay? Would she swim today?

"Why are you thinking she won't?" I wondered out loud.

Ji Hoon (who was sitting on my left) turned to me. "*Mwo?*" He gave me a funny look and I realized I had spoken my thoughts audibly rather than in my head, to myself.

I shook my head, signaling that I meant nothing, but he did not let it go.

"*Geunyeoneun nugu-inga?*" he demanded, his voice taking on a tone as slick as a snake. "Who is *she?*"

"My mother," I quickly improvised, avoiding eye contact with him and gazing out at the water in front of me instead. I hoped he did not sense my nerves shaking inside of my voice. "I wonder if she will be okay. She has not been doing well lately – hunger pains."

Ji Hoon nodded in agreement with me, leaning toward me to whisper in Korean, "Do not let Byung Hun hear you. He will write down what you say if he discovers you. Your words undermine the Supreme Leader and his ability to provide for us."

This guy was absolutely right, and I noticed he was trying to protect me. Maybe Ji Hoon was not so much of an asshole after all.

At the mention of the swim team's minder, I stole a skittish glance in Byung Hun's direction. It relieved me to see that the man was so busy talking with one of my fellow swimmers that he did not even pick up his name, despite Ji Hoon's inability to actually keep his voice at a low level. His version of whispering reminded me of my grandfather's definition of the type of talking when he started to lose his hearing.

A smile grew on my face at the thought of my grandfather. He would be so proud to see me here. My abeoji *and* my halmeoni both! I must dignify my family name with any medal, if not gold. I hoped it was gold, though, naturally.

My thoughts were interrupted when I noticed two Americans walking toward the poolside. It was Sloane and *that girl*, Chloe, and I now believed that they were on good terms, as they were walking closely. The anger I saw between them before did not flood their vision or their faces like it did last night.

Sighing with a sense of alleviation, I put my hands on my knees and braced myself to watch my girlfriend swim. Would I shout out loud for her as she competed? I truly wished I could. Hopefully, she knew that I was thinking about her and believed she could do anything.

At that moment, Sloane peered up into the stands, obviously searching for me. When our eyes met, she waved at me, a coy expression splayed on her face. *The least* I could do was return the gesture, so I did, attempting to hide my hand between my legs and toward my feet.

Unfortunately, Byung Hun must have noticed, for he leaned impolitely across three other swimmers between myself and him and did not bother to whisper to me the following words

"*Bakke nagaja.*"

My legs trembled underneath me as I followed my minder down the stands toward the exit, thoughts of uncertainty tearing through me like a tornado. Before we went through the double doors, I gazed back at Sloane in despair. Would I get to see her swim or would I miss it? That was all my mind could think about at this moment as I tried to shut out what would happen to me next.

Once we entered the deserted hallway, my minder did not hesitate to grab my arm tightly, his fingers digging into my skin.

"*Ah pa!*" I cried out involuntarily as my brain registered the pain. Yes, I should have kept my mouth shut, but I could not help it.

"*Mahaljima, yaeya!*" Byung Hun commanded, his voice harsh yet quiet at the same time. ("Do not talk, boy!")

Byung Hun glared at me from his short stature. Even though he was not as tall as me, I was still afraid, for he had big power. The power that this man had was one that could destroy my family and myself with just one word to Kim Jung Un.

Hmmmm, I thought observantly, *That's the first time I have not referred to that man as The Supreme Leader!*

I did not have time to digress in my thoughts, for Byung Hun slapped his hand heavily on my shoulder. "Who is the girl you are waving to?" he asked me in Korean. "What is your relationship with her?"

"I was just being nice, sir," I fibbed willingly, looking down at my feet out of respect.

My heart raced as I realized that I needed to get back into the pool area in order to watch Sloane swim. If I did not go now, I would miss her send off.

"I must go back in," I whispered, my voice barely an audible octave.

Byung Hun opened his mouth to say more as he attempted to clutch my wrist, but I was heading toward the doors that lead to the competition with such fierceness that I knew he would not catch me in time. Surely he would not act abusively in front of the public, either. Therefore, I was safe out in the stands. At that moment, I decided I would sit a little away from this man, on the other side of Ji Hoon, to make sure he could not reach me as well.

Running into the room, not caring who noticed my overly brisk movement, I pushed my way into the stands just as the fog horn went off and Sloane and the other athletes dove into the water.

I did not even glance over at Byung Hun, but I could feel his eyes burning a hole into my face.

The other North Koreans did not notice, gratefully, for they were so engrossed with the meet.

What would happen to me next? I couldn't help but wonder as I watched Sloane power her way through her competitors one by one, taking the lead. *What will happen to my family?*

My heart still had not calmed down; it was thundering in my chest like lightning bolts hitting the ground. This was it – my future, my family's future, was at stake now. Even so, I could not keep away from Sloane. I would not. She was my new future, I decided suddenly. Did I want to go with her simply because I was in trouble now? Maybe that was partially something to do with it. If I looked back at all of the illegal equipment my family and I had, though, at all of the outlawed things I had done so far while in Beijing, at the thoughts that had been going through me lately…I knew that I did not want to be in North Korea anymore.

What would it take to get out? Many had tried…and died. Any effort to leave the country by ship, plane, walking, or another form of transportation without a permit was deemed to be punishable by placement in a prison camp, death, or another form of punishment. Would my parents even want to leave? My sister? What if it was just me?

As Sloane ended her race, her outstretched hand touching the wall, I jumped to my feet, no longer caring. I was in trouble already, so why not get into more?

"Yes!" I shouted out loud in English, warranting shocked whispers and gasps from my fellow North Korean swimmers sitting next to me.

If I was going to go down for loving someone who was not North Korean or for not being focused solely on my sporting mission at the Olympics, then I might as well go down with a fight. A fight for the girl I loved – Sloane. She was worth the cost.

CHAPTER NINETEEN

Sloane

Splash! My head hit the water, and I immediately started working my arms like the machine that I was. No worries about who was in the lead, no thoughts about what was going on in the stands or elsewhere, no inquisitions about whether or not the other girls I was swimming against were better than me. My body did what I had designed it for long to do – it swam. And it swam well.

My thoughts were laser focused, and I didn't have a single stray speculation deter me from my one purpose at this very moment: Win a medal. Jae Sung's image held strong in the back of my mind, but at this moment, it was on the back burner. I would have to worry about him later...

At that moment, though, my mind immediately drifted to him. Look at all of the pain I had caused, just by wanting to meet him. God knew what was going to happen to him now. Should I continue to meet him? Would I even be able to?

For a brief second, I lifted my head to see where I was. My heart seized in my chest when I realized that I was at least a good three feet in front of Chloe and as for the other swimmers – I was definitely further than them. All that mattered was that my hand touched the wall first.

Pumping my arms like I had never done before, I reached the first turn around, and I gracefully did a flip in the water, using my feet to propel myself forward toward the opposite direction. My lungs burned in my chest, but I ignored their plight as I used every ounce of determination left in me to keep. On. Going.

Surprisingly, I could hear cheers from the stands as I came up for air each time. That spurred me on a little bit more, my desire to gain an Olympic badge of honor pushing me further and further. All of my training came down to this one moment.

So, I *did* care if I won, after all. In fact, I *did* care about it, despite having feelings for Jae Sung.

For some reason, I was shocked to discover that the two desires could coincide with each other. My parents couldn't come to the Olympics to watch me swim because my dad (who is a heart surgeon) had a huge surgery scheduled that couldn't be put off, for fear of the patient's life, and my mom…she didn't have a full-time job (except for taking care of and running our home), but she had neighborhood luncheons to attend as the HOA president. Yeah, that was it.

I had Jae Sung. And Susan. That was enough. They were rooting for me. I wondered if Jae Sung was able to cheer me on out loud from the stands or if that would get him in trouble. Was he even *back* in the stands or was he talking to his minder? Was he *allowed* to come back into the arena? I couldn't wait for midnight to talk to him…if I was even *able* to see him tonight after what had just happened.

Finally, this was it! My hand touched the wall the fastest I had ever touched it before, and I popped up out of the water.

"Yesssss!" I screamed with all of my might, knowing without a shadow of a doubt that I had come in first.

Just to confirm my uncertainty, I peered up at the giant monitors above the pool. My name peered back at me in full force, seeming to pulsate in the harsh lights on the ceiling. Gold: Sloane Austin, USA! Yeeessss!!! I didn't contain myself *at all,* shouting once more and jumping up and down in the pool. My last name didn't mean "great" for nothing!

Chloe had touched the wall shortly after me, meaning she had won silver. We high-fived and then actually *hugged* each other! Things and people *can* change and no matter the differences or the past, I learned right there that all that matters on a team it that you *support* your teammates. Differences and disagreements aside, we were there to back each other up. From this day forward, our relationship would change, I realized.

Remembering my boyfriend, I stared up into the stands, hoping to catch him sitting there. My heart broke out in song when I noticed he was back in the stands. Had he been able to see my entire meet? As quickly as my spirit soared, it was deflated like a pierced balloon when I noticed the look on his face. He was actually scouring, which was odd because I hadn't seen him do that this entire week. Surreptitiously, I glanced at his minder and found him giving Jae Sung a look of equal measure.

Oh no, he was surely in trouble. And I had caused it all. Shame filled my soul, and despite my recent win, I couldn't help but feel awful. Actually, that word doesn't even describe the depths of worry, fear, and remorse that I felt. I had to fix this, but how? Was there any way?

Jae Sung stole a glance in my direction, and he gave me a small smile and a thumbs-up, not even caring to look over at his minder to see if he had noticed. That indicated to me that his minder knew about us. Would it all go downhill even further from here?

No sooner had I lifted myself out of the pool than Chloe and Susan approached me. Chloe had obviously been out of the pool for a minute, because she had a towel wrapped around her already.

"Hey, let's go talk to the reporters!" Chloe urged. Susan surrounded us with hugs at that moment too, the pool water from my body dripping down her blue jeans and onto her Team USA T-shirt.

With one more nervous peek back at Jae Sung, I made my way to the reporters, who were obviously from NBC. Would my mom and dad see this on TV?

"Sloane, that was an amazing swim!" one reporter encouraged me, a pearly white grin on her overly botoxed face. "Tell us about it!"

Putting on a happy face, I let the reporter and whoever was watching know that I had just gone out there and given it my all, putting my training into practice. I thanked my parents for persuading me to get into swimming in the first place as well as Susan for her great coaching.

Deep within my heart, I kept thinking about Jae Sung, unable to avoid my anticipatory dread.

My win was hampered by the reality that he would probably face a gigantic problem from our relationship.

The gold was worth it. Was this connection I had made worth it as well?

CHAPTER TWENTY

Jae Sung (재성)

All I could think about was her. Sloane. As my team, my minder, and I exited the building, I made sure to steer clear of my minder as much as possible, pressing my body closely to my fellow swimmers.

My minder's eyes bore into me from behind, and I could feel his desire to speak more with me. How would I avoid Byung Hun's further acquisitions? What was going to happen next?

Would my parents and the Supreme Leader be notified, and if so, what was going to happen to me and my family?

All I did was try to support someone, I thought rebelliously with an obvious frown spreading across my face. *What is so wrong about that?*

The whole time in Beijing, I had been questioning everything I was taught from my country. In North Korea, we are taught to listen to our parents and elders, to follow the directions of our government one hundred percent without question, to obey our police force no matter what they tell us to do. Yet a little time away from my homeland had taught me so much already.

Was it Sloane's fault I was having these thoughts? Not at all. I had already rebelled with my secret items stashed away back at home. Those would be enough to get me into the utmost amount of trouble. Yes, my mother knew about my illegal contraband, but my father did not. In fact, my eomma had given me strict orders *not* to tell my abba that I had such things. Thankfully, my father had not searched my room, which was something that happened often in so many homes in North Korea. Families would turn against families out of fear for being imprisoned for the particular family member's indiscretion.

All I wanted at this present moment was to be free to do what I wanted, when I wanted, without the scrutinization of those in authority over me. I wanted to be myself, to like who I liked, the very same things it seemed so many athletes from various countries at the Olympics were allowed to do...but us from the Chosun.

It felt like my mind was creating a new pathway – one that would forever change my future. If I was sure to be in trouble with my minder, I would definitely be in trouble with my parents *and* my government. This would mean that I could not go back to my home country...I *would* not go back.

How would I escape? How would I get away? The minder was with us all of the time. Yet, I had managed to get away at night to the rooftop in order to meet with Sloane. If I could do *that*, surely I could get to the American Embassy in Beijing. It would have to be at night, though.

When I got there, what would I say? If I left North Korea, I would be leaving my whole world for my entire eighteen years on this earth behind.

What would happen to my parents and my sister? It was a risk I had to be willing to take. Was it selfish? Maybe. I could only hope that they would be able to escape before something so torturous came upon them due to my offenses.

The plan was set in motion, then. I would attempt to get to the American Embassy tonight. If Sloane was with me, perhaps she could help me? I did not want to endanger her as well. Upon reading about China, I discovered that they were similar to North Korea in many ways – one of the most significant similarities was that they had a law enforcement like ours called The People's Police. These men and women would patrol the city, and many North Koreans had been caught by them and sent back to my country just to face public execution, torture, imprisonment, or death. If they caught me and discovered I was North Korean, I knew I would face trouble.

Perhaps I could dress like a South Korean? I had seen enough prohibited movies from the south that I knew what the men there looked like. But where could I get the clothes? Maybe Sloane could help with that as well?

I was leaning a lot on my new girlfriend that I had only known for a few days…yet my feelings for her were so strong. I had never felt like this about anyone. Ever.

If she was in the same predicament, I knew with certainty that I would help her in any way I could. Would she do the same for me?

"Would you all like to go out to eat for lunch?" my minder asked us all in Korean, putting on a smile, which I had never seen him do at all in the months that I had known him.

Our team had not been out to eat at all since we got to Beijing because the Supreme Leader gave us a strict budget. Therefore, we each brought our food from home in a separate suitcase. Perhaps we were given some funds to spend on at least one day of food, though.

Everyone agreed that it would be nice to eat somewhere, maybe even get some Chinese food.

Would I be able to sneak away at that time, to get to the American Embassy in broad daylight? No, it would be easier at night.

Surely the place would be locked up at night, though. Would I be able to sneak in and stay the night there until it opened the next day? Maybe Sloane had a phone and could look up the information for me tonight. While we were allowed cell phones in North Korea, they were highly supervised, and I had not brought my family's phone from home.

As I looked around at my teammates, I realized that this would be the last time that I would see many of them. Tonight, I would be making my journey to freedom.

CHAPTER TWENTY-ONE

Sloane

"**H**eyyyyy," I greeted my mother in a sing-song voice as her phone picked up on the other line. It had been at least a week since I'd talked to her so her voice sounded foreign to me.

"Sloane!" my mom shouted, causing me to hold my cell phone a little bit away from my ear. "We stayed up to watch your competition. Wow! You did an AMAZING job, sweetheart!"

My dad said something unintelligible from the background, and my mom let me know she would put him on speaker phone so I could hear him.

"Way to go, Sloane!" my dad cheered me on, surprising me.

He had definitely done one-eighty since our talk in front of the swim store, which seemed so long ago. It felt good to have *both* of my parents on my side!

"It was a hard swim," I acknowledged for the first time, breathing a sigh of relief. "I'm just glad my part for Team USA is over."

My mom humphed out loud, letting me know she disagreed. "*Your* part may be over, but your teammates' parts aren't. Don't forget to support them, as well, until you come home."

My mom had been a cheerleader in high school and college, so she understood the importance of being a team player. My dad? Not so much. My parental units met at Dartmouth College, my dad a biology major on track to become the surgeon he is today, and my mother was studying to be a teacher. Mom served as a teacher after I was old enough to enter pre-kindergarten, but she retired early at dad's suggestions.

I was shaken out of my deep thoughts by my mom's urgent voice. "Slooooane," she drew out my name, which let me know she had been talking, and I was ignoring her. A common fault of mine, I guess. "Have you met anyone? Made any friends?"

A lump formed in my throat. Would I tell my mom and dad about Jae Sung? I could hear the lecture now. *You aren't at the Olympics to meet boys! We sent you there to compete!*"

"There's this girl, Grace, that runs marathons," I informed my parents, sliding by the one person I *wanted* to bring up to them. "She's from Orlando, Florida. We haven't gotten to see each other much because we both have been busy with our individual sports and training sessions, but we met on the plane because we sat together. I will definitely keep in touch with her when she gets back because she is actually going to go to Boston College in September!"

My dad barked out his approval from the background. Phew. Would he approve of Jae Sung?

It's now or never…let's find out. I must've been asking for punishment.

"And…..there's a boy….." I offered, not sure how to begin this conversation.

My mom inhaled before speaking. "Okay. You know you're there to swim, right? Of course you do, sorry. Well, tell us about him. Are you being safe?"

I rolled my eyes at that. They meant were Jae Sung and I having sex and if so, were we doing it safely? Apparently, the Olympics Committee offered free condoms to all athletes at the event.

We hadn't gotten that far yet, which was perfectly fine. I couldn't bring myself to imagine having sex on top of an open roof with nothing but a couch. God knows who'd sat on that couch besides us, even. And I didn't know him well enough yet. I wanted this to develop slowly.

"We haven't even gotten to that yet, Mom," I replied in a low tone, trying to hide my annoyance. "We just talk. It's been nice getting to know someone and I really like him."

At that moment, my dad asked the question that I knew would come up: "Where is he from?"

My heart didn't ask if it could start beating rapidly. It just did. Forcing myself to breathe and wiping my sweaty palms on my jeans, I asked myself if it was best or necessary to tell my parents the truth at this point and about this topic.

I had never lied to my parents before. Yes, I was not your typical teenager. While others around me went out to party until God knows when and got into drunken car accidents and experimented with drugs and dated around, I was busy working on getting into the Olympics. Also, I didn't want to disappoint my parents and my coaches.

"He's from a Northern Asian country," I primed my parents with an offhanded reply.

My mom's voice rose several octaves, letting me know that she was on to me. "Oh really? Would that country be North Korea?"

Now or never. Now or never.

"You guessed it right," I acknowledged my mom's answer with a deep sigh of relief.

No matter what they said now, I had done my part. Still, I was curious as to what sort of feedback my parents had about my admittance.

"Sloane!!!" my dad screamed so loudly it felt like he was in my dorm room with me. "You know that country is dangerous, right?!"

I was so glad that no one was in the room with me, but at the same time, I was worried about someone coming in and overhearing my conversation or passersby catching onto my words.

"Dad," I whispered back to my father, hoping my calm demeanor would bring his temper down a notch. "It'll be okay. Truly."

"No, it won't, honey," my mom sided with my dad. "That country doesn't allow their citizens to do much, and many of them hate Americans."

I could feel my own temperature rising, but I forced it down as I clenched and unclenched my fists at my sides. "Mom and Dad, this guy is different. He actually has stuff that he's not supposed to have, like a computer, and he wants to be a doctor."

Maybe that last part would pacify their fears. "Sloane, I don't care what you say this time," my dad retorted, and I could almost picture him shaking his head at me like I was a little kid again. "This guy can be dangerous for you. China sends North Koreans back all of the time if they're caught, so I'm surprised they're allowed to be at the Olympics this year. If you're caught with him, God knows what will happen."

SO that was that! I would have to hide my meetings with Jae Sung from my parents…and everyone else. Thankfully, Chloe had promised she wouldn't tell anyone about our late-night appointments.

This was so disappointing to me, though. Out of all of the people that I wished I could tell about Jae Sung, my parents were number one.

However, what did I think would happen?

Would I truly be able to meet up with Jae Sung when we were in college? Would he be able to fly to America to see me? Most likely not.

At that point, I deduced that it would be best to break it off with him, no matter how strong my feelings for him were at this point. No one else had ever made my heart flutter like being with Jae Sung did. Having deep conversations with an eighteen-year-old guy wasn't heard of in my lifetime, and he was one in a million to me.

Tonight. I would let him know on the rooftop at midnight, I decided wistfully. No matter what I wanted, this was one argument I obviously could not win with my parents, the government, or anyone else.

CHAPTER TWENTY-TWO

Jae Sung (재성)

Lunch was over, and now, it was time to show what I had been working at for so long. It was time to use all of my practices, every competition prior to this moment, each moment I had envisioned the gold medal in my hand in order to achieve what I had worked so hard for. It was time to make my country proud.

My teammates and I entered the swimming pool area only to find there were not very many people there. My heart dropped from disappointment in my chest. Yes, we were not a very popular country, as I had found out from many late-night Google searches on North Korea from my illegal laptop. However, I projected to myself that people would want to come see us out of curiosity at the least.

As my team filed into the stands, I headed toward the pool, shedding my clothes and placing them next to my bag by a wall. I was flanked by five athletes from other countries who were joining me for our competition – Monaco, Maldives, Malta, San Marino, and Bermuda. As I warmed up my arms and legs, I silently sized them up, judging their bodies compared to mine. *They are at least twice my size*, I realized with a sinking feeling. Hastily, I turned my thoughts around to remind myself that I was a strong competitor who was trained in this sport and size meant nothing if the execution of swimming moves were not precise. One could be skinnier and smaller (like myself) and yet, if their moves were perfect, they could win any competition.

I was interrupted from my thoughts and my stretching with the blow of a whistle, which signaled us to take our spots on the diving platform. As I stepped up on the box, pulling my cap onto my mat of jet-black hair, I looked hopefully into the stands. *Would she be there?*

The guy from Malta caught my gaze and shot me a dirty look. *Well, that just fueled my desire to beat him.*

"Welcome to the 2008 Olympics Men's Freestyle Swimming competition. Today, we have...."

I drowned out the announcer's voice and wishfully searched the stands but found that Sloane was not there, sadly. I allowed myself to wallow in self-pity for exactly one second. *Maybe she is busy with something. I will see her tonight.*

A Team USA jersey passed by my vision just as I was pulling my goggles over my eyes, and I looked over again to see that Sloane had in fact joined the audience! Immediately, I felt my heartbeat accelerate with excitement.

We exchanged smiles as she sat down by herself in the stands. All I needed was *one* fan, and she was it. Yes, I had my country's teammates, but this girl had come to watch me and she wasn't even from North Korea. That meant the world to me.

Sloane gave me a thumbs-up and I nodded at her, carelessly forgetting that my minder could be watching me but honestly not giving a single care to the notion of trouble.

I pulled my goggles on hastily and leaned down in my diving stance, ready to take on this competition. The whole room was silent, waiting with bated breath to witness the takeoff.

The whistle blew and I jumped swiftly from my diving platform, my arms and legs instantly springing into action. I was in a tunnel of my own making, oblivious to the athletes on each side of me. In my head, I chanted: *Gold medal, gold medal, gold medal.*

The water rushed up to meet me as my body worked, gushing around me like a plastic mold. I pushed hard, my heart beating soundly in my chest. When I came up for air, I could hear the chants and cheers and encouragement resounding from the stands, thrusting me further. I trained my mind to focus on the applause of my fellow North Koreans, and I searched for Sloane's acclamations. Happily, I discovered both and used that as ammunition to continue on the journey.

As I approached the wall, I made my turn effortlessly and began my trek back to the finish line. It was at that moment that I began to feel some tension in my arms.

I willed my arms to hold on, sending silent messages to them to obey my efforts. *Oh no! Were they giving out on me? Do not do this now, arms! Come on! Do what you have been prepared to do — take me to the gold! Ttong!*

Curiously, I took one look at how far I had to go. Just two meters left. *I could do this!* Even though I had been trained *not* to look at the other athletes, I allowed myself one glance to see where I was at. Malta was on my right side and was slightly behind me, so I thanked whatever power was in the heavens. On my left, Monaco was making their way to go head-to-head with me. I *had* to push myself a little more if I wanted to stay ahead of him.

With one final thrust, I tagged the wall. *Was it good enough?* Eagerly, I popped up in the water to look up at the monitor, which displayed our swim times. *Was I ahead of Monaco, of all of the other athletes?*

I WAS IN FIRST PLACE! YES! GOLD! GOLD! I DID IT! THIS WAS WONDERFUL!

With a ten-second lead, I beat Monaco!

Sheepishly, I glanced over at the guy from Monaco, who threw me a sneer. I returned his look, then turned my body in an effort to ignore him.

Grinning from ear to ear, I gazed across the pool at Sloane, who was now standing on her feet, clapping. We exchanged smiles, and I knew that I could not *wait* to talk to her tonight!

"Jae Sung Kim, first place, North Korea!" the announcer called out over the loudspeaker.

Reporters rushed to the poolside, thrusting microphones in my face. I could not even get out of the water before I would have to speak. *Was the Dear Leader seeing this in North Korea?* I knew that regular North Korean families would not be seeing this because most did not own a television. Also, all that was played on our televisions (without illegal mechanisms to get programs from other countries) were messages and shows from the government about our leaders.

"Jae Sung! Jae Sung! You did it!" one reporter with fiery red hair shouted.

"Yes, I did," I replied, stealing one more glance at Sloane before pulling myself out of the pool. I was ready to get my gold, but first, I had to meet a pretty girl at midnight.

———◇———

My heart beat with anticipation as I entered the rooftop at midnight. I could not wait to see Sloane and tell her my plans and talk about my swim! Our nightly ritual had become an oasis for me.

At the sight of Sloane standing at the edge of the balcony, her hands gripping the ledge as she peered out over the lights of Beijing, the desire I had to feel her lips on mine grew. It felt like I had not seen her in multiple weeks instead of hours.

Hearing me arrive, Sloane turned around, her sapphire-blue eyes catching my dark, coffee-brown ones and lighting up immediately. We ran toward each other and our bodies crashed into each other as if they were one. *An explosion of desire.*

Hungrily, I placed my hands on each side of her face and brought her mouth crashing onto mine. Sloane's mouth opened for mine, and my tongue immediately moved to taste hers fervently.

I felt my hands warm up as they stayed stuck to her beautiful face as Sloane wrapped her arms around me in a tight embrace, pulling us even closer to each other. Our mouths would do the talking tonight, at least for now. It was like a meeting of one's true self, my soul joining with my body for the first time ever.

Breathlessly, she moved her hands down my back and my torso until they reached the top of my pants. Involuntarily, I let out a low moan, which caused a smile to break through our kisses. Sloane's hand dipped between my skin and my clothes, and I felt it slip around the firmness between my legs.

In my country, we are adamantly informed to never engage in any sort of sexual activity before marriage. If my family knew about what was happening up on this rooftop in another country, I would be in so much trouble. Chastity was a thing of virtue in North Korea. Even so, I am convinced that many couples do have sex, but do not talk about it. It is a thing that is ignored and denied, like the true feelings so many of us have about our governmental leaders.

Wordlessly, Sloane and I moved toward the couch, my body effortlessly falling on top of hers. We did not show any concern for the fact that someone could easily enter the rooftop at any moment and catch us. All that mattered was being together.

I moved my lips down her neck, gently caressing her buttery skin with my lips. This was the first time I had ever done anything of this sort with any girl my age. Was that something I should bring up to Sloane? Would it matter that I was a virgin? Were American girls generally more experienced than their Asian counterparts?

Her eyes boring into mine, Sloane lifted her white Team USA T-shirt over her broad shoulders and tight midframe and heaved it onto the concrete floor. I could not take my eyes off her. Every inch of her was gorgeous, including her black lace bra. Sloane took that off too, revealing her generous breasts underneath. I felt myself harden even more down below.

There were no reservations on either of our parts. It was clear that we both wanted this. I had no doubt that we would not regret this either.

I matched Sloane movement for movement as we shed layers of our clothing until we were both completely naked. We both took a moment to look longingly at each other's bare bodies, delighting in what we saw.

Smiling warmly back at Sloane, I climbed back on top of her. "Are you sure?" I whispered in her ear before kissing her neck.

"Yes," was her simple reply, moving her hand to grab my ass firmly in its grip.

I hated to talk about the next item at hand, but I needed to before we engaged in anything further. "I do not have a condom."

Sloane shook her head, a nonchalant look splayed across her pretty face. "That's okay. I am on birth control."

Birth control. In my country, it was regulated so much that only married women were legally allowed to have it.

I took her last response as a final okay. As I entered her, our bodies becoming one, Sloane whispered sweetly in my ear, "I love you, Jae Sung."

I found myself wanting to say it back. "I love you too, Sloane."

How was it that we had found each other like this? Where had she been all of my life? I wanted nothing but to make her happy... especially tonight. Her pleasure was of utmost importance to me.

With every thrust into her small frame, I felt my body relax from the tension it had amassed earlier. Leaning back, I gazed into Sloane's eyes and she peered back at me. Her face contorted into a look of pleasure, which mine matched.

With a final groan, I released all I had into her and fell, gasping, on top of her. That was the most wonderful thing I had ever experienced before in my life!

We both had no words at the moment. All we could do was stare into each other's eyes. I scooted up behind Sloane and wrapped her body against mine, my arm splayed across her breasts.

Kissing her ear, I murmured, "*Saranghe.*"

"What does that mean?" Sloane looked back up at me, grinning from ear to ear. Her face was flushed a light shade of pink, and as if it could be possible, she looked alluringly lovely.

"I love you," I translated for her, placing my lips over hers and giving her a hearty kiss.

CHAPTER TWENTY-THREE

Sloane

So that just happened. No going back now.

We only had a few more days with each other, though. It was highly unlikely that we would have time to have sex after this week in Beijing.

My heart *was* soaring, but at the thought of not seeing Jae Sung after this week, it flopped to the ground. I knew right there that I did not want to be apart from him. Yes, I was young. Yes, I hadn't even graduated from high school yet. My maternal grandparents were proof that you could meet your soulmate in high school, though.

How could we be together? He would go back to North Korea, and I would never be allowed to see him again. Americans are not allowed to legally enter the northern part of the Korean peninsula.

At that moment, it was like Jae Sung read my mind because he said, "Sloane, I have an idea."

I felt my palms go sweaty with anticipation and my heartbeat sped up. "What is it?"

Before he answered, Jae Sung got up and put his clothes back on. I followed suit, figuring it was silly to be the only naked person up on this roof.

After we dressed, we sat side by side, our knees touching. Jae Sung took his hands gingerly in mine, turning to face me on the couch.

"Your swim today was amazing! Both Malta and Monaco were gaining on you, but you pushed through!" I absentmindedly ran my fingers through his thick black hair.

"My arms almost gave out," Jae Sung admitted, hanging his head. "I cannot believe I won!"

"You are an amazing athlete, so I'm not surprised," I admonished him, a smug smile on my face.

He leaned over and kissed me gently, silently thanking me for my support.

Jae Sung took a deep breath and let it out, which signaled that he was about to say something to me.

"I would like to go to the American Embassy to try to ask for asylum," he informed me, his voice level and taking on a serious tone.

Woah! That was a plot twist to our story that I never saw coming!

Would he be able to make it to the embassy? From the videos I had watched about China, I knew that The People's Police patrolled every inch of this country 24/7. How would Jae Sung get there without getting caught?

"You will have to travel by night," I thought out loud. "That's the only way you won't get caught."

Jae Sung agreed with me with a nod. "I also thought that I could see your cell phone to see what time the embassy opens?"

I wasn't aware that he didn't have a cell phone of his own, but that made sense. We had taken out my cell phone to view pictures of my parents, my dogs, my city, and other points of interest in my life on numerous occasions together this week. Yet, I realized I hadn't seen *his* phone. "So you're not allowed phones?" I asked, genuine curiosity peeking inside me.

Jae Sung shook his head, a somber look coming across his face. "We are not allowed many things, including electronics. I have a secret laptop at home that I use, and my mother knows about it, but not my father."

I took a deep breath and let it out to slow my breathing down. "I was so worried about you earlier. I saw what happened in the stands. Could you tell me more?"

Jae Sung proceeded to tell me how his minder had seen him cheering for me and that he was pulled into the hallway and threatened. He was sure that this would get back to Jim Jung Il, which would most definitely result in his own death or imprisonment, as well as that of his family's.

I felt so terrible. If I hadn't met Jae Sung, none of this would have happened! Guilt flooded my soul.

"I am so sorry," I apologized, tears sliding out of my eyes and falling steadily down my face. "I caused this."

Jae Sung ardently shook his head, leaning over to pull me into a strong embrace. "This is not your fault. If anything, it is mine. I am the one who gave you the note."

Leaning back and looking into my eyes sternly, Jae Sung added, "But I regret nothing."

I couldn't believe this guy would risk his life, his future, his whole livelihood and that of his family's on me. One girl. Yet that was what love was, wasn't it?

"I'll do anything I can to help you," I offered, pulling my phone out eagerly and sliding closer to Jae Sung on the couch so he could look at the screen too.

I quickly found the American Embassy's address and website. It took us a while to find the information, but we were both disappointed to discover that the embassy didn't open until 7:00 a.m. How would we possibly get there without being seen, if we wanted to move at nighttime? In addition, the building was brand new, just completed this month of August, so it might attract a lot of attention.

"I have a solution," I offered. "How about we leave right now, and we hide somewhere near the embassy until it opens?"

"That sounds good, except for the fact that there will be Chinese guards all over the place. How will I bypass them?" Jae Sung queried, fear pricking his heart and mind immediately.

"That's a good question," I affirmed, chewing on my bottom lip with worry. "Also, I've heard that if North Koreans are caught, they are sent back to North Korea by the Chinese government."

Jae nodded his head solemnly. "That is true. The only reason we were allowed to come into this country was for the Olympics. We are not allowed to leave the Olympic complex."

I didn't know that. Shock filled me to the core. This was a dangerous, incredulous situation. How would we get Jae Sung to that embassy?

"Do you believe in God?" I asked him, hope heavy in my voice.

He took a moment to respond.

"I am not certain if it is the same God as my grandmother, whom she called Jesus, but I am beginning to believe there is a bigger thing out there than me," he admitted. "I believe something or someone led me to you."

I agreed out loud with him. Our meeting was not by circumstance or luck or chance.

"I told my mom about you today," I offered, a shy grin blossoming on my lips.

"Oh? What did you tell her? That I am handsome? Smart? Funny? Amazing?"

"Something like that." I leaned over to give him a kiss.

"By the way, you did *simply wonderful* swimming today! Congratulations on your gold, *babe*," Jae Sung praised me, emphasizing the word "babe."

"Thank you," I whispered, not wanting to discuss the matter of getting my boyfriend to the American Embassy any further but knowing we needed to do so. Time was of the essence. Peering at my watch, I shockingly discovered that it was already 2:00 a.m. We had been on the rooftop for two hours and the North Korean swim team would be continuing their competitions in about five hours.

"We have to get you to that embassy," I just about whined, my mind going into overdrive. "I have a couple of dark colored hoodies in my trunk back in my room. I could go get them, then we could go over the side ladder and climb our way down."

"Will people not miss you if you are gone?" Jae Sung questioned, his jet-black eyebrows raising to his equally raven-colored hairline.

"Of course. But I can let them know that I wanted to explore the city a little, since my job is done." I fidgeted with a hangnail on my index finger.

"Okay," Jae Sung whispered. "I hate putting you in the middle of this."

"You can't do anything about it," I retorted, pulling him closer to me. I rested my head on his chest, feeling comfortable through and through. "I'm already involved. You can't get rid of me."

Jae Sung laughed out loud, and it was the most beautiful thing I had heard all night. In fact, I don't think I had heard him laugh much in the past couple of days.

"Wait here," I ordered him, standing to my feet and stretching a little before heading to the rooftop door. "I will be right back with the hoodies, then we will be off."

Jae Sung only nodded, nerves revealing themselves on his face.

"It'll be okay," I reassured him, before disappearing into the darkness of the stairwell.

CHAPTER TWENTY-FOUR

Jae Sung (재성)

I waited on the rooftop for what seemed hours, fear and concern taking a toll on my mind as I fought off worries. What was taking Sloane so long? Had she been caught – by my minder or her coach or team? By her friend or the girl who was previously her enemy?

Just as I was about to get up and go after her, not caring about the cost of doing so, the door to the rooftop swung open, and Sloane quietly came back out. In her arms she held two hoodie sweatshirts, one navy blue and the other black. She also had a map of some sort, most likely one of Beijing. Good planning.

Without speaking, we both put on a hoodie and pulled it tight over our heads. Our eyes bulged wide in our heads as we made our way to the staircase.

"This is the last chance to leave," I warned her. "I could do this on my own."

"What kind of girlfriend would I be if I let you alone?" Sloane replied, actually giving me a wink.

Girlfriend. We had not used that term (or boyfriend, for that matter) this whole week. Then again, neither had we used the words "I love you" until tonight. This was getting serious…and I did not mind it at all.

"I love you," I said again, the words fresh and sparking something new in my heart.

"I love you too," she matched my words.

Before we headed down, we both peered over the side of the rooftop, scanning the grounds surrounding our dormitory and the surrounding dormitory for guards or police officers. Seeing there were none, we both sighed with relief, then squeezed each other's hands as a sign of support and hope.

Sloane slung her leg over the side of the rooftop and placed her feet on the metal ladder that clung to the side of the building. She placed her hands on each side of the ladder, positioning herself to start going down.

Neither of us knew if this thing was sturdy or not. More dread filled my gut, and I warned her to be careful as she started making her way down.

"We got this," was her simple response, her head down and focused on each rung of the ladder. Step by step.

I started to follow her down when I heard the rooftop door swing open. My eyes nearly fell out of my head as they took in none other than Byung Hun, entering the blacktop area.

"Go, go, go!" I whispered feverishly to Sloane, praying silently to the new god I now completely believed in to keep us safe.

Sloane must have heard the door open too because she started pumping her legs swiftly, her hands moving just as fast as we made our descent.

Our swimming lessons and coaching had paid off for this instance.

Would Byung Hun hear us on the ladder? What if he started to come down and tried to catch us?

With an amused smile playing on my lips, I recalled that Byung Hun was not a small man. He had obviously enjoyed one too many dinners provided by the government's assistance…while so many of my fellow countrymen and women starved. It would be near impossible for him to catch either Sloane or myself.

I could not tell if Byung Hun was walking around above our heads, and I did not slow down to listen. Just as we both reached the bottom, however, I looked up and saw him peering over the side! Our eyes met, and he started shouting what could only be obscenities at me, his face twisted into one of utmost rage.

Taking my hand, Sloane pulled me away from the building. We ran toward the entrance to the gate surrounding the dormitory villages, not bothering to look back.

After we ran through the complex entrance, we both hid our bodies behind a thick pillar, leaning against it for support. We did not need to catch our breath so much as we needed to stabilize our minds.

"That was close," my girlfriend whispered, turning to look at me with a scared expression.

I simply nodded my head then replied, "But he could never catch us! Did you see how big he was? He has had one too many kimchi pancakes!"

We both laughed out loud, forgetting that we were now not in the safety of the dormitory.

Sloane pulled out the map and we studied it for a moment, finding the place where we currently were and marking a route to the American Embassy with a pen she had obviously brought.

"We will stay in the shadows. Don't walk near street lamps," she advised.

When we got to the embassy, what we would do, I did not know. All I knew was that I could see my freedom and it was almost in my grasp. And it was all thanks to this beautiful American girl who had already changed my life in the course of one week.

CHAPTER TWENTY-FIVE

Sloane

Something shoved my shoulder hard, startling me awake. "Sloane!" I heard a girl calling my name loudly like I was sitting far away from her. In fact, I was sitting right next to her.

Spooked, I bolted upright in my seat and took a look around, my eyes nearly bugging out of my head. What in the world? Seriously, why was I on a plane and not in the helicopter with Jae Sung?

It all came back to me. I was heading to Beijing to compete in the 2008 World Olympics. That meant...

That meant that....that meant that....oh my gosh....meeting Jae Sung never really happened....it was all a dream....no way!

NO! WAY! THIS had to be a dream! I HAD met him! It felt so real! Everything that happened was TRUE! My head spun with a slam into reality.

I looked up at my friend, who was peering at me with wide eyes, obvious concern plastered across her face.

"Are you okay, Sloane? You look like your dog just got run over," she tried to make a joke, but I didn't laugh.

"Are we headed to Beijing right now?" I whispered, barely able to get the words out.

"Duh. In fact, we only have about thirty minutes left in our flight. Wow, that must've been a really deep dream," Grace replied, replacing her worried look with an amused smile stretched across her lips. "What did you dream about? Was there a boy?"

I rubbed my eyes and sat up straight in my airplane seat, still dumbfounded that all of *that* could've been a dream. The way it felt to kiss Jae Sung, how my heart skipped a beat when we held hands, keeping our relationship a secret, Jae Sung's stories about his family and life in North Korea, running to the American Embassy, getting in a helicopter to cross to America, falling asleep with my head on his shoulder...all of that...*wow, all of that*...it wasn't real.

My heart broke, and I found tears sliding out of my eyes involuntarily. I put my head in my hands and tried to breathe in and out deeply.

"Sloane, do you need me to get your coach?" Grace offered, placing her hand on my shoulder as her demeanor passed back into fear.

I shook my head. "No, it was just a very interesting dream, and I can't believe it wasn't real."

In psychology my senior year of high school, I learned that the mind is more powerful than we think. It can create new ideas and dimensions and worlds even while we are sleeping. That must've been what happened to me.

Not wanting to be bothered, I sat back in my seat and closed my eyes. Grace must've gotten the idea because she sat back in her seat too, though when I opened one eye to peek at her, she was still gazing at me in fear.

"I'm fine," I reassured her, even as I knew I was trying to convince myself as well.

Frantically, I searched my memory for information Team USA had learned about in regards to the countries that would be at the Olympics this year. Was North Korea going to be there? Honestly, I couldn't recall. My best bet would be to ask Grace... but she might think it was a funny question to ask. Here goes nothing...

Blowing a deep breath out, I turned in my seat to face Grace, playing with the hem sleeves of my Team USA windbreaker. "Grace, is North Korea going to be at this year's Olympics? I can't remember."

Grace didn't hesitate to give me a strange look, which gave me my answer even before she spoke a word. "Yes, but why?"

My thoughts intruded into our conversation. Jae Sung was fake. My dream was fake. The love I felt was fake. I felt my heart shatter into two pieces in my chest, and the tears began flowing like a steady stream.

"Sloane, I am really worried," Grace confessed, taking my hands gently in hers. "What is going on? Please tell me. I can only help if you let me know."

I felt so alone in what I had experienced.

Maybe it was best to share with someone else about my dream, regardless if they thought I was crazy or not.

For the next thirty minutes of our plane ride, as we made our descent into Beijing, China, I poured my heart (and my delusional fantasy) out to Grace. I watched her face transform from surprise to joy to concern all in one sitting.

"I wonder how your mind came up with that," Grace thought out loud at the end of my deeply personal share. *I wondered if she thought I was crazy...*

I didn't know. What I *did* know was that this had happened for a reason…as crazy as it all was, I was supposed to get something from it.

All I could think about was Jae Sung. If he wasn't real, I knew North Koreans were. What would I do with the information? As soon as we got to the Olympic Village, I would pull out my phone and Google information about North Korean human rights violations. Then what would I do with it? I didn't know just yet, but I knew this was the start of something.

Mom and Dad wanted me to be a doctor, but I was always interested in justice. I can recall being as young as five years old and constantly calling out my classmates for various infractions against one another and the teacher, ranging from stealing each other's crayons to writing on their desks. There wasn't an elementary school report card that didn't have comments like, "Sloane is an upstanding citizen," and "Sloane is always standing up for fairness in class."

Maybe that's what I would do – major in something internationally related and work in the United Nations or some other committee that could help North Koreans.

I could see the idea taking form in my mind: Working with a civil rights organization or defending refugees. This would be honorable, though it wouldn't win my parents' approval. In fact, their disapproval would be written all over both of their faces, I knew that for sure.

One thing that dream did, though, was shake me up. Right then, I decided that I would not live for anyone else's dream but my own. My major would be something that would help others less fortunate than myself, and I knew that I would want to experience Asia outside of the realm of my sport and the Olympics one day.

At that moment, the captain came on the speaker and made the announcement that we were preparing to land in Beijing within the next few moments. He rambled on about the places you could do some sightseeing and the weather. Yada yada yada.

The seatbelt chime rang out, waking me up from my thoughts. *Ding!*

I jumped out of my seat, eager to get my bags, wondering if I would see Jae Sung after all. Maybe he *was* real? What if he was South Korean or Chinese instead of North Korean? What if he *was* North Korean?

The thought was so crazy. So crazy it could be true. More insane things have happened, right?

My mind fixed on the movie *Sleepless in Seattle* as I flung my Team USA carry-on bag over my shoulders, absentminded to whomever it might hit.

"A little impatient, are we?" Chloe muttered from her seat across the aisle from me, throwing me a scathing look.

"Don't do that, it makes your face look uglier," Grace piped up beside me.

I stifled a laugh as I waited in line in the aisle to deplane. One thing that hadn't changed from my dream: How rude Chloe was. Although…I reminded myself that she had become nice after she discovered Jae Sung and me.

As I walked down the aisle to get off the plane, my heartbeat sped up and so did my thoughts, if that was even possible. I couldn't *wait* to get to the Games to see if Jae Sung was real or not!

CHAPTER TWENTY-SIX

Jae Sung (재성)
North Korea

Impatiently, I shifted my foot from one to the other. "*Eoseo haebwayo*," I thought to myself, ready to start the Opening Ceremony already.

I am a swimmer for Team North Korea, born and raised in Pyongyang, the capital. Swimming has always been second nature to me, something that I have loved to do. My parents used to joke that I am a *mulbakk-ui in-eo,* a "Mermaid Out of Water."

My parents never sought the limelight, though. In fact, they try to stay out of it as much as possible. It is not good to show too much pride in anything but your country. Everything we have ever done is for our homeland. My parents have always supported my dreams and goals, though.

Though they may not have their own, my parents know the importance of dreams. Their dream was to one day travel outside of North Korea...while mine was to win a gold medal for my country's honor.

Sometimes I felt selfish in the light of my parent's dreams, but they reminded me that it was important to be who I am and follow the path that The Great Leader laid out for me, whatever that may be. I would not be at this Olympic Games without my parent's support, I knew that much.

My trip to Beijing was a way for my parents to live vicariously through me. Until they could travel as well, I would swim for them too.

In just two weeks, I will be starting at Kim Il-Sung University in Pyongyang, with a full swimming scholarship as a member of their swimming team. I could see myself majoring in something like International Affairs, one day being able to travel again outside of North Korea on behalf of my great country. Had I told them that yet? No, but I would.

For now, I was focused on my pursuit of the gold. I had been training all my life for this one moment. Well, it *felt* like all of my life, but in reality, it had been just twelve years, since I was five. My mom enrolled me in my first swimming program at the Changgwangwon Health Complex.

The moment my head hit the water, I was completely enamored with all things swimming. By the next year, at the age of six, I joined my first swimming team, and in middle school until now, I had always been on a school swimming team. It was my life.

The Games announcer broke into my thoughts to let me know that we were set to start the show. Finally!

China went first, as they were the hosting country. Next was Yemen, then a few other Western countries. Finally, North Korea was called, and I gave a rounding "*Aegukka!*" with my teammates, our fists raised in the air.

We made our way through the tunnel, following the South Korean flag. As we entered the arena, my eyes were blinded by the lights – both from cameras and the stadium.

I could not believe it! After so long, my most important dream was coming true! This was it!

Were my parents watching? Was my country watching? Our country usually did not allow anything to play on the television except for programs about our government. However, this was a special occasion and Eomma and Abba promised that they would try to tune in if the show was broadcast in North Korea. The idea that my parents would be watching gave me an exhilaration I had never experienced. It felt like I was soaring in the clouds like a bird, circling high above the grass.

After walking the length of the circle in the center of the stadium, my teammates and I took our place next to the Netherlands and waited for the United States to come out next.

I found my heartbeat accelerating for some reason. Why? Well, I had always wanted to *go* to the United States. I reassured myself that maybe *that* was why I felt like this.

As the United States entered, my eyes zeroed in without asking on a pretty brown-haired girl in the middle of the pack. Tall, slim, definitely a swimmer's body.

Surprisingly, she looked back at me too! A look of shock went across her face, then a wide smile broke out. It was as if she knew me...and I felt like I knew her too. Strange. I had never felt like this before. It was an uncanny sense of déjà vu that I was feeling at this moment.

For some reason, I wanted to run to this girl and meet her immediately. All thoughts of *why* I was here and any swimming dreams I had were forgotten. I *had* to meet this girl!

As the ceremony trudged on, I felt myself becoming more and more impatient. When could I go over and introduce myself? And would I be allowed to or would I be whisked off with my coach and my teammates after the ceremony ended?

Finally, when I thought I would scream because I could not take it anymore, the show ended. The announcer made their announcements and without asking, before I could hear a word from anyone in my country's party, I tore over to the United States team and went directly to the girl I had seen. The girl I now could not stop thinking about this whole time since she entered the same arena I was in.

My minder definitely saw me go to this girl, so I was a little worried. Also, would this cost me my chance to swim? Regretfully, I realized then that I had acted before thinking.

As I approached, however, I noticed her face was shining with anticipation. If her smile was any bigger, it would have stretched her face by twelve inches. This put me at ease and allowed me to push the thought of being in some sort of predicament to the back of my mind.

"Hi, I am Jae Sung," I offered, sticking out my hand.

Her mouth dropped open at my introduction.

For what, I did not know?

"Hi, I'm Sloane. It's good to meet you," she replied, shaking my hand.

This was the first time I had met this girl, yet it did not feel like that. It felt like I was meeting an old friend, one I had met back in grade school. This was different. It was like my soul knew her soul. It is hard to describe, but that is the best way to interpret how I was feeling and what I was thinking at that moment.

Surprisingly, more than swimming, more than anything I had ever wanted in this world and in my lifetime, this felt right. At least at this moment. It felt like my body had found its actual home.

"We have a lot to talk about," Sloane said as she passed me a piece of paper that had her room number in Olympic Village on it.

"Oh? Would you like to meet up tonight, if I can get away from my team?" I offered, staring deep into her eyes.

I watched her face shine brighter at my request. "I would love that. How about the rooftop of my dormitory in the Olympic Village, building three?"

That was an odd request to me. The rooftop? Why not the lobby? Hastily, I shook the odd feeling off, as I reminded myself that my minder and teammates could not spy on me at the top of a building...unless they followed me there.

"That sounds great."

We just stood there, awkwardly staring at each other, not knowing what to say next. Even so, there was an electric-type magnetism that floated invisibly between us. Though I could not see it, I could feel it humming through my whole body. It was an unseen string tying me to Sloane already.

"Sloane, come on! A bunch of us are going out to eat!" a tall girl with platinum-blond hair in a ponytail came jogging over to us. She threw me a strange look that I tried to ignore.

"Jae Sung, this is Grace," Sloane informed me, posturing herself between us. "Grace, meet Jae Sung."

Grace replaced her wary look with one of curiosity and excitement. "Hey! Good to meet you! I've never met anyone from North Korea!"

"Now you have," I joked back, trying to break the stiff feeling suddenly drifting around in the air.

"I'll see you tonight, Jae Sung," Sloane ended our time with a simple wave. Her eyes told me she wanted more than that.

"See you tonight," I murmured toward her as she departed. *Who was this girl?*

CHAPTER TWENTY-SEVEN

Sloane

I had met Jae Sung, and he was North Korean! Wow! I couldn't believe it!

It felt so weird, though...it was a sort of déjà vu. He looked exactly the same, he talked just like the Jae Sung of my dreams, and the attraction was obviously there between us.

Would our meetings be the same? Would we kiss, and if we did, would it feel the same way?

What would we talk about? Were all of the stories about North Korea from the Jae Sung of my dreams true? I felt like I was back at square one.

Also, the gold medal...not true. I didn't win one...yet. I knew I could do it, but to do it again...I was already tired thinking about it. The feeling of the push off, using all of my skills I had obtained through countless hours of swimming practice, racing someone to the finish line – that had already happened for me. I would have to do it again, and I was doubting if I could or not.

The door swung open, interrupting my worried thoughts. Jae Sung stood in the doorway, looking at me up and down. I threw him a small smile, welcoming him onto the rooftop with me.

He took a small step toward me, then another, and before I knew it, we were hugging. It felt so good...like my soul was back in my body. I wrapped my arms tightly around him, forgetting the sounds of the city below, the lights of the buildings surrounding the one we were on, forgotten behind my eyelids shut tight.

"Was it hard for you to get here?" I asked, wondering if he could understand what I was saying.

Jae Sung confirmed that he did, indeed, understand English, as he responded, "No. In fact, I am in the same building as you."

I leaned back in his arms and took in his features, studying them in order to commit them to my memory. Chiseled chin, square jaw, thin eyebrows, chocolate-brown eyes. All the same.

How would I tell Jae Sung that I dreamed about him? Should I? Would he think I was weird or crazy? How would I begin to tell him that I knew who he was?

"Why do I feel so connected to you?" he asked, guiding me to the couch that was (surprise) actually the same one of my dreams.

We sat down next to each other, our legs touching, a warmth spreading up my thighs. I placed my hands in my lap, tearing at a hangnail as apprehension flooded my heart.

"What if I told you we have been here before?" I almost wondered out loud, turning to face him.

Cautiously, I peered into his face, searching for signs of distrust, fear, or concern. Thankfully, I didn't find any. Instead, I found a look of interest splayed across his face instead.

"I would want to know more, of course."

Sighing, I took my hand in his, readying myself to share with him that I had actually dreamed about him. Instead, I asked him, "What is the craziest thing you've ever done?"

Jae Sung laughed out loud, a giddy smile crossing his lips. "Well, not many, as we have a government that cares for us. They do not want to see us do crazy things."

Crazy things? This Jae Sung was definitely different from the one of my dreams. I quickly reminded myself that the one I met initially was naive at first as well, and over the course of our time together, he changed into a more open-minded guy. Would that be the case with this version of him?

"Okayyyyy," I replied, drawing out my reply so that I could think of a way to rephrase my question. "What would you say was the most unexpected thing you've ever done?"

Jae Sung slid even closer to me, slinging his left arm around my shoulders. I took note of the muscles in his bicep, which were brushing my back. Strong, well-knit. Hot.

A blush creeped across my face as I waited for Jae Sung to respond to me. It felt like forever.

"Well, between us, I have a laptop that I should not have. In North Korea, only the government and certain soldiers may own a laptop," Jae Sung confided in me, dipping his head low to mine.

I could smell the shampoo in his hair – it smelled like natural rain water. A field of grass. Without wanting to seem like a total weirdo, I inhaled slowly but a little more deeply.

"Wow, that *is* unexpected," I confirmed, nodding my head to show agreement. "Well, I have something unexpected that happened between us. I...Well, I...Sort of dreamt about you before we met."

Jae Sung raised his eyebrows sharply, his face taking on a funny look. I expected him to bolt right there. Instead, he let out a loud laugh, throwing his head back against the couch. "Really?! That *is* crazy!"

My heart sank to my feet. Oh no. I knew this would happen. I prepared myself for some rejection just as Jae Sung continued –"Well, I am glad it is not a dream and that we are right here, together, in real life." Jae Sung touched my chin, his fingers warming up my face, which was chilled to the fifty degrees of the outside air.

"Me too," I agreed, leaning my shoulder down into his chest. Pushing closer and closer.

"I would like to kiss you, but that is not something that we usually do in my country." He studied my lips like they were a school exam he needed to pass.

"You are in China right now, though," I reminded him, turning my body so it was facing his instead of side-by-side.

He nodded a verbal acknowledgement, then leaned his face close to mine. I could smell his breath now – it was minty. There was a woodsy smell to his skin, and I wanted to taste it.

Our lips touched gently at first, but then harder. I slipped my tongue into his mouth and his met mine eagerly, tasting me.

We wrapped our arms around each other, locking in a full embrace as our hands explored each other's bodies freely and hastily. It was me who pulled away.

"Let's take it slow," I requested, trying to catch my breath.

"I would like that. So, tell me about your city, Sloane." Jae Sung let out a small laugh, then he slid back into a side-by-side position with me on the couch.

For the next few hours, we talked about everything under the sun. When I felt my eyes were starting to close, I decided it was time to go back to the room and get at least a few hours of sleep. My first practice would be today, and I needed to be rested for it.

"Do you want to meet here every night, at midnight?" I asked almost too eagerly, hoping that it wouldn't scare Jae Sung off.

"Yes, yes, I would love that. See you tomorrow, Sloane."

My heartbeat picked up in my chest, and I gave Jae Sung a warm smile. "See you tomorrow, Jae Sung."

CHAPTER TWENTY-EIGHT
Jae Sung (재성)

When I got back to my room, I noticed that one of my teammates was up, reading a book about The Dear Leader. The lamp on the nightstand next to his bed was on, but the others were able to sleep, somehow.

"Dong Hyun, *ajigdo mwhohae*?" ("Dong Hyun, what are you still doing up?") I snuck a glance toward our minder, Byung Hun, who was thankfully still asleep, snoring away on his bed.

"Don't you worry, Jae Sung. I will not tell Byung Hun about your little nighttime excursion," he replied in Korean, closing his book and turning in his bed to look at me. "So long as you share your secret with me."

Should I tell him? Was he trustworthy? If I was not allowed to see Sloane, if I was not able to even talk to her, and if Dong Hyun told our minder and he told the Dear Leader, that may lead to me being kicked off of my team and sent home, or worse, I would be killed or put in a gulag.

"I wanted to see the city lights." The lie went down my throat like a hard rock. I swallowed, forcing it down to the pits of my stomach.

Dong Hyun raised one eyebrow, judging what I had just said. "Are you sure about that?"

"Why are you so worried about me? You do your thing and I will do mine, man."

I could tell that this guy would not let it go, that he would continue to press me, but I did not have the strength to fight anymore with him. Instead, I turned my back on him and climbed into my bed across the room, facing the wall, and willed sleep to meet me.

What would I do if Dong Hyun found Sloane and me together? Would we get in trouble? We did not discuss at our team meetings back in Pyongyang what we should do when we met a foreigner.

It took what felt like forever for me to fall asleep, my mind circling with thoughts of fear.

Would I be willing to risk my life, the possibility of a medal, the ability to stand on the platform as one of the top three finishers in my sport, all of that – for a girl I had just met?

Yet I knew deep within my heart that there was something pulling me toward this stranger turned acquaintance. I could not stop seeing her…I had to see what this was.

I fell asleep to the thought of Sloane's face in my mind, analyzing her every feature.

CHAPTER TWENTY-NINE

Sloane

"**P**ush! Push!" I heard the chants from my teammates and my coach as I came up for air during my practice.

This practice felt more like a pre-competition. I was swimming laps in the Olympic pool, but there were reporters, fans, and other countries flanking the poolside. In the pool with me was Germany, England, Australia, and Japan. Big hitters.

I successfully rounded at the wall and made my way back to the other side, my arms pumping as I swam breaststroke to the finish line. What I loved the most about freestyle swimming was that I could do breaststroke, but I could also do a backstroke, a butterfly, or a sidestroke. Anything I wanted to. The breaststroke was my favorite, though.

As I neared the edge of the pool, I noticed Germany gaining speed on me. *Oh no you don't*, I silently scolded my opponent, pushing myself even harder. My hand met the wall just seconds before theirs.

"A little friendly competition, ja?" the girl from Germany asked me, turning to smile at me.

"Gotta get ready for the Big Day somehow," I responded, shooting her a smile back.

My morning had been kind of hectic – I had slept through my first alarm. Susan (my coach) became my second wake-up call, shouting my name and demanding that I get up. I bolted out of bed and rushed to get breakfast from our mini fridge and the coffee pot – oatmeal, a little coffee, and off we went.

It took me a while to fall asleep because all I could see was Jae Sung's face in my mind. The conversations we had. The kiss. It lingered inside of me, taking residence in my heart. He was here, he was real, and we were going to be together.

A little nerves kept me awake, honestly too.

This was my first Olympic competition, and I wasn't too sure of myself. I had studied the other athletes in my field during registration, and they all looked strong. Quickly, I reminded myself that I was strong too. This practice showed that.

As I climbed the ladder to get out of the pool, water dripping down my body, I turned my head to look into the stands. Yes, I expected that Jae Sung would be there…and I was right.

At the moment, he was engaged in conversation with a teammate. When I turned to him, though, he turned to me, and our eyes met. We both gave each other a little awkward wave.

This Jae Sung was a little less cautious than I imagined. He didn't stop to look at his minder to see if he was watching his every move. I liked that.

Thankfully, though, his minder wasn't watching. He was engrossed in conversation with a team member behind him, fully turned around in the bleachers. Thank God.

Pulling my swim cap off my head, I gave Jae Sung a wide smile, then headed for the showers. I couldn't wait until tonight.

CHAPTER THIRTY

Jae Sung (재성)

"What did you want to be when you grew up?" I asked Sloane, slinging my legs across hers and leaning back against the armrest on the rooftop couch.

We were lying on the couch at opposite ends but facing each other, our legs laid across one another's. It had been a few days since we had been meeting, and a number of practices after we first met. This nighttime practice of meeting each other on the rooftop had become common and felt comfortable already, even in a span of less than a week.

The night sky tonight was almost a velvety purple, emblazoned with a million stars as if a blanket was pulled over it. I had seen similar skies to this in Pyongyang, but there was a mandatory "lights out" at about 9:00 p.m., so one did not see as many building lights as you could see here in Beijing. Each of the lights clumped together like one big halo, illuminating the darkness. It was magnificent.

"When I was little, I always wanted to be what my parents were – they're both doctors. Now, I think I want to do something to help others, like work for a non-profit." Sloane traced her nails down my arm, sending a ripple of goosebumps to my shoulder and back. "What about you? What do you want to be?"

I closed my eyes, allowing myself to still for just one moment. "It is not as simple as that. My duty has always been to serve my country, my government, my leaders. Since coming to China, I have learned that I want to do the same as you – but I want to get out of North Korea."

Sloane sat up when I said these words, propping her elbows on the couch, solemness covering her face. Even with the frightened look that she now wore, she was beautiful.

"Why? What makes you want to leave?"

I chewed on my bottom lip, pondering her question and how to answer. What *made* me want to leave? I knew the answer shortly after hearing her query.

"I cannot do anything without the government knowing. I cannot breathe. Also, if I want to travel, I have to get a permit. We North Koreans cannot just *leave* our country anytime we want to."

This was the first time I had spoken those words out loud. Wow. They hit me like a freight train, going ninety miles an hour. So this was it – I wanted to leave North Korea. I would be leaving behind my whole family, and who knew when they would be able to join me?

Being in Beijing had awakened something in me, though. Seeing people from all over, being able to go where they wanted to and when, it inspired me. Sloane had motivated me as well in the short time that I had known her. Why could we North Koreans not have the freedom to go anywhere and search the Internet and watch TV shows about whatever we wanted to without getting into trouble? These were questions I would not *dare* think out loud while in Pyongyang…but here, in this other country, I was free to wonder.

Sloane sat up all of the way now, taking me into her arms. "In my dream, I helped you escape to the American Embassy. Maybe we can do that again."

Her suggestion stirred up something in my chest. Encouragement, excitement, acceptance. "We should do it."

But how?

"But how?" Sloane wondered out loud, matching my thoughts.

As we twined our fingers together until we looked as though we were one, we talked about different ways we could get to the embassy: The ideas ranged from realistic ones (sneak at night and hide away until the morning, then walk into the embassy) to ridiculous notions (beat up two guards, dress up like them, and walk to the embassy).

Suddenly, Sloane's blue eyes blazed bright. "I got it!" She snapped her fingers together, mouth gaping open in surprise. "I can befriend or flirt with a South Korean swimmer, work my way into his room, steal his jersey, and use his passport to get us to the embassy! We could go after we have both completed our competitions, so our main obligations would be done."

Pursing my lips together in deep thought, I nodded my head in agreement. "This makes sense. Though…the idea of you flirting with another guy is not very tempting to me, I must say."

I winked at her and slid her close with my arm, burying my nose and mouth into her neck. There, I gave her gentle kisses that sent chills down my own spine.

She wiggled away from my nuzzles, but firmly grasped my hands in hers. "We will leave once your competition's over, since you swim after me. It'll be much easier with a passport and a team jersey from South Korea – no one will suspect that you are North Korean!"

At that, I *did* find myself a little wary. When my teammates and I were checking into the Olympics, I had taken a moment to size up the South Korean players. They were a little bigger than me.

"Could you possibly get a jacket too?" I requested, hoping that I was not asking too much of my new girlfriend. "The South Korean players are a little bigger than us, and taller. I at least need something to make me look a little thicker."

"I'll try," she promised, leaning forward to plant a small but sweet kiss on my lips.

This was it. I would be leaving everything I knew behind for the chance at freedom. The cost? My family, who may face death. As I pondered this, I felt my heart sink. This was hard because I did not want to leave my family to possible doom.

However, I knew that I wanted to live in liberty. Maybe I would be able to bring them over once I had arrived? We would see. All I could do was pray to whatever god was out there that they would be safe until I could help them from my own place of security.

This was such a dilemma, but it was one I was willing to take. Until now, neither me nor my family had taken a trip outside of North Korea. We deserved to be able to do so, though. I knew that now more than ever.

CHAPTER THIRTY-ONE

Sloane

This was it. THE BIG DAY. I had been preparing for this one moment for what seemed like a lifetime. Even though I had definitely been distracted by Jae Sung, I was still ready for this competition, more than ever. This was what I was created to do – swim. Today, I would be swimming for the gold, nothing less, nothing else.

As I made my way to the locker room, nerves shot through my body from head to toe. I willed myself to calm down, taking deep breaths in and out of my nose. Setting my gym bag down on the nearest bench, I leaned over to untie my shoes. At that moment, Grace came up, slapping me hard on the back.

"Oof!" I let out a grunt, straightening my back. "Gee, thanks!"

"That was a good luck slap!" Grace informed me, drawing me in for a big hug. "You're going to do great!"

"Speaking of great, how was *your* race?" I asked, pulling away from the hug and putting my gym bag and my overclothes in the locker while I talked. "I wasn't able to see the medal ceremony this morning, sorry. It was a rush getting here."

Grace tugged on her white Team USA T-shirt, revealing a swatch of ribbon beneath her shirt. Grinning from ear to ear, she pulled out a big, shiny, gold medal, which was almost bigger than her hand.

"I did it! I got first place! But man, it was a close one, Sloane!" Her voice held all of the excitement I hoped I had *if* I medaled gold. *When, I mean.* "Austria was close to me, within seconds! I thought I would for sure take a silver instead of the top place! At the last moment, though, I pushed my legs hard and made it over the finish line…completely by a nose! So crazy!"

I high-fived her, my enthusiasm level rising. "That's awesome! Way to go! That inspires me to go out and do my best, friend."

Grace gave me one more quick hug, then swatted me on the ass. "Get going! You're going to do the same – just watch! You got this!"

I nodded solemnly, willing my own belief in myself to catch up with my friend's expectations for me. *Did I have this?*

One more time, I peered into the mirror. I wasn't worried about what I looked like. Instead, I needed a personal pep talk.

Remember when you were little and you wanted to swim? This is your dream – don't let anyone take it from you!

There we go. I felt one thousand times better. Mom always said, "If no one can lift you up, no matter how hard they try, it's your turn to lift yourself up."

As I walked the hallway toward the pool area, I swung my arms, stretching them at the shoulder. Once I approached the pool area, I pulled on my cap, goggles, and worked my legs and arms a little, feeling my body come to life.

This was it.

I stepped up to the pool, with Belgium on my left and Japan on my right, ready to take my first competition on. At that moment, I heard loud cheers coming from the stands. My American teammates were rooting for me, boosting my confidence even more.

"Welcome to the Women's one-hundred-meter freestyle competition," the announcer boomed out over the loudspeaker. "Today, we have Belgium in lane one, the USA in lane two, The People's Republic of China in lane three, Japan in lane four..." The announcer finished his introductions while I tuned him out, trying to focus on the upcoming competition.

Four whistle blows signaled that we should get up on our podium. I jumped in, turning around and gripping the silver handles in my wet hands. I knew the drill.

Before I crouched down and got ready to go, I allowed myself to look up at the North Korean team in the stands. Though he hadn't called out or made a noise for me, as I locked eyes with Jae Sung, I noted that he had a trained smile on his face.

That was enough to tell me that he was rooting for me... within his mind. I knew it wasn't safe for him to shout for me, but he would if he could. The smile was all the ammunition I needed to complete this swim successfully.

The high-pitched whistle sounded, kicking me into motion from my place on the platform. I dove into the water, arms and legs stroking back and forth immediately. My body knew what it was doing after hundreds of practices, and it swung into motion easily. The water lapped around my ears, welcoming me like an old friend.

Wall coming up. Turn approaching. Turn complete. As I swam back toward the finish line, I lost track of the people around me...

Until I heard the loud chants for Japan resounding in my ears as I came up for air. They were growing louder and louder by the moment. Even though I knew I shouldn't, I peeked over to Japan, now on my left. This girl was fire! We were literally neck and neck, and I had to do something about it or I was going to be going home with a silver instead of the top medal!

Come on, Sloane. You are better than this.

No one deserves this gold more than you. Get going, girl! Keep it up! PUSH!

Athletes know more than anyone else that ninety percent of a race or even a workout is self-talk. If you can't convince yourself that you have what it takes to win, *who can?*

Willing my arms to obey my positive thoughts, I forced myself a little harder. *Just a little more and you're there!* I looked over at Japan just as my hand smacked the wall.

She had smacked the wall…right after me? Before? She was now treading water. I would have to wait for the results to be displayed on the television on the ceiling.

Please, I whispered to myself, breathing hard in and out as I tried to bring my heart rate down.

"In first place, we have Sloane Anderson, Team USA! She came in first by just three seconds, ladies and gentlemen – what a race!" The announcer delivered the sweetest words I had ever heard in my entire life…*except for the name Jae Sung, of course.*

I trained my eyes on the screen and saw that I had come in at a time of 48:06, with Japan just behind me at 48:09 (*what a close one*). Russia was in third, with a time of 48:25, which was behind Japan and me, but not by much. *What a race!*

Racing again, I got out of the water and hugged Susan and Grace, caring only a little bit if I got water on them. They obviously didn't care, because they both embraced me tightly and gave me high-fives. My teammates came down from the stands and surrounded me, patting me on the back.

Jae Sung and I met each other's gaze again, and he gave me a thumbs up, which was something I had told him meant "good job." He didn't know any signs of encouragement that Americans use before I let him know that a thumbs up would suffice.

As I exited the pool area and made my way around the cordoned-off walkway, tons of reporters called my name. I chose to speak briefly to one from ESPN.

"How do you feel, Sloane?" she asked, pointing her microphone in my direction and flashing me a toothy white grin.

"Tired," I admitted, still trying to calm my heart down. *Inhale, exhale.*

"I bet you are! First place! Way to go! If you could say anything to anyone, what would you say?" she raised a perfectly clipped brown eyebrow inquisitively.

"Mom and Dad, I did it! Now, I can play!" I joked; my unknown thoughts trained on Jae Sung.

The reporter laughed along with me, and I excused myself to go to the medal platform, where the ceremonies for the gold medal were about to take place.

As I stepped onto the first-place podium, I felt a shot of pride for my country shoot through my veins. I had done my job…it was hard, but I did it.

Now, I could sit back, watch Jae Sung swim, cheer him on, and help him get to America.

CHAPTER THIRTY-TWO

Jae Sung (재성)

She had medaled! Sloane did it; she got a gold medal! I was almost more excited for her than I was for myself!

Was the gold worth it, seeing as I was going to try to get into America in a few short days? I decided that yes, it was. I had worked my whole life for this, and I did not want to give it up. Before, I had been swimming for the glory of North Korea.

Today, I was swimming for myself. That was okay, right? It was not selfish? I decided that if it was selfish, that was okay, as I had literally never done anything for myself…well, except for sneaking an illegal phone and a banned laptop into my bedroom back in Pyongyang. But that benefited my eomma as well because we would watch pirated South Korean dramas on CD. Swimming for a gold medal was legal, so it was different.

It was my turn today. *Would I win a gold?* I did not know, but I would try. Most of the guys my age had many advantages over me – they were bigger in weight and height, and I guessed it was because they ate more. One look at them during meal times in the cafeteria at the dormitories told me that.

Eagerly, I put my outerwear in my locker along with my gym bag and my tennis shoes.

Stripping down to only my jammers (which are tight-fitting swim shorts), I carried my goggles and my cap with me as I made my way down the tunnel toward the pool.

Last swim and you are done. You can do this, man! Do not give up! Work hard!

Trying to calm my nerves, I took deep breaths in and out my nose as I noted the athletes I would be swimming against today. I was in the middle of China and Australia. Though both guys looked substantially bigger than me, I knew I could beat them. *Skills, not size, matters.*

"Welcome to the Men's fifty-meter freestyle swim. In lane one, we have China. Lane two, North Korea. Lane three…"

As I listened to the announcer go on, I swung my arms back and forth, stretched them overhead, and worked my legs a little. The whistle blew, signaling it was time to take my place.

I forced my nerves to the pit of my stomach.

Use those nerves to push you through this, Jae Sung, I could hear my halmeoni reminding me.

Taking one last deep breath, I took my stand on the platform. My coach handed me a bucket of pool temperature water, and I poured it over my head in an effort to prepare my body for my swim. That initial shock always got me, but the bucket water was helpful.

I bent down, readying myself for the moment I would leap off the platform. *This was it. This was it. This was —*

"Take your mark."

The whistle went off, and I dove as far as I could off the platform, propelling myself into the water with my arms and legs. My body immediately beat at the water around it effortlessly as I willed my ears to go temporarily deaf to the boisterous chants and cheers resounding from the stands.

No time to look to my right or my left, only time to trust that I was going to take the gold. I pushed myself to the brink just before my hand touched the wall. *Was it good enough?*

"Our winner is – Jae Sung Kim of North Korea! This is a first, folks! Look at this!"

I craned my neck up toward the television and my eyes fixated on my name, firmly set in first place. I HAD DONE IT. GOLD. GOLD!!!!!!!

Breathing deeply in and out through my nose and mouth, I willed my heart rate to slow down. *Eomma, Abba, I did it! I did it! Are you proud?* I was surprised that my thoughts were on making my parents proud, not my country. That was enough for me to realize right then that I did not want to remain in North Korea. I loved my family, but I did not love my country, like I was trained to do for my entire life.

As I exited the pool, I realized I had not even looked at Sloane the entire time. I was so laser focused. Guilt flooded me as I peered up into the audience, only to find her face and our eyes blazed into each other's. She gave me a small thumbs up, puckering her lips up as if kissing me. I let a small laugh out in response.

This girl was becoming a part of my world, and it had only been a few short days. I had completed my first mission, now I was ready to take on my second and third – being with her and getting to America.

People called my name from all around, most of them reporters. As I stopped to answer questions, I had one question in mind: *Though I was successful at winning gold, would I be just as fortunate to be able to escape North Korea?*

CHAPTER THIRTY-THREE

Sloane

Call me "Stealthy" because that's my new name. Over the course of the day, I had slowly worked my way into the inner circle of the South Korean female swim team. My goal? To find out which guy was the most desperate...and he had to look like Jae Sung, of course, or our plan wouldn't work.

Just when I was about to give up, I met Seo Yeon (a female swimmer from Ansan) as we both walked toward the cafeteria for dinner. She was the sweetest – and the most gullible. I hated duping her, but it had to be done. This was the *only* realistic way that I could help my boyfriend get into the American Embassy.

"Soooo, I really want to meet a South Korean guy," I began, giving her my most friendly smile. "I think they are so hot! Can you introduce me?"

"Sure, sometime I will," she offered, giving me a shy smirk as we walked toward the cafeteria.

I shook my head adamantly, signaling that that wouldn't do. "I need to meet a guy *today!*" Okay. I knew I sounded desperate, but desperate times call for desperate measures.

"Girl, you have another two weeks here, you know? You can take your time, you know?" Seo Yeon blew her bangs out of her eyes. "Did you come here only to meet guys?"

"You know it," I joked. "Just call me a Man Whore."

Whatever it takes.

Seo Yeon laughed along with me, but I noticed that her laughter was a little more forced. "Okay, sure. Well, there *is* one guy. The first is Sang Hoon, over there." She pointed toward the buffet line, and I noticed a big guy, hearty, who looked like he could lift a rhino with his bare hands. "He is a weight lifter. Yes, he is big, but he also has a big heart."

She was *really* selling it. I wonder why?

Was he coming onto her or something and she was trying to deflect him to me? Still, he wouldn't do. He was too big...I needed someone with a swimmer's or a runner's body.

"Not my type," I swiftly informed her, scanning the room for a more applicable "victim." "What about that guy over there?"

I pointed toward a guy who was surrounded by a group of friends, laughing like he had not a care in the world. He looked like the type that would *love* to brag to his buddies back home about how he *bagged* an American girl at the Olympics. A real douche. He was worthy of this con.

Not only was he deserving of handing over his passport and some Team South Korea memorabilia unknowingly, he looked a *lot* like Jae Sung. In fact, if I squinted, I could almost say they were twins. Same chiseled chin, similar jaw line, a carbon copy of my boyfriend. *He would do.*

"He's not really that friendly of a guy," Seo Yeon murmured, her lack of confidence dripping with every word she spoke.

"Watch me turn that around," I said confidently, quickly getting up and making my way over to Mr. Unfriendly's table without a second thought to my actions and their possible repercussions. *This was the only way.*

Putting the sexiest look I could come up with on my face, I threw my arms around the guy, who sat unexpectedly back in his chair like he owned the place. "Heyyyyy," I crooned, locking eyes with him.

Jae Sung sat across the cafeteria from me, and I knew he was there. I shifted my gaze to look at him momentarily and almost ruined the plan. He looked like a boy who was sad because he lost his puppy. I winked at him to let him know I was doing this all for him, and his face broke into a smile.

Training my eyes back on the guy in front of me, I whispered, "You wanna go back to your dorm?"

"It's that easy, huh?" he responded, looking around at his friends for their manly support. They bellowed out laughter in response, high-fiving him.

Yes, he was a douche. No regrets.

"I guess it is." I traced his ear with my lips.

I trained my mind not to care about who was watching or what they were saying, but I could feel what seemed like a thousand heads trained in our direction. It was like being back in the high school cafeteria when someone asked you out to prom.

"Let's go," he practically yelled, taking my hand and leading me toward the exit doors.

As we went out the door that faced the dormitories, I threw one last glance back at Jae Sung. "We got this," I mouthed to him, hoping he could read lips.

Once we got into his room, this guy actually thought he could start kissing me. I gave him the impression, though, so I wasn't exactly a saint here. His hands got a little too frisky as well, and I pushed them down next to his sides.

"Let's slow down a little," I offered, backing away from him with my hands up.

"You said you wanted to see my room. Well, here it is. Now, what's next for us? You know why you wanted to be here. Your room looks the same as mine..." he rambled on.

How would I get him to leave me alone for five minutes so I could get his passport and his outfits?

"I, um, suddenly don't feel well," I whispered, touching my forehead and letting out an agonized groan. "Do you have any Tylenol and a wet washcloth? Could I lie down for a while?"

The guy stared at me, his eyes becoming big saucers on his face. He looked frozen, as if he didn't know what to do. "Um, sure...I have two sisters. It must be your time of month."

"Maybe it is," I murmured, thinking, *Jerk.*

Mr. Not-So-Nice-Guy slinked toward the bathroom in the corner, and I took that chance to inch my way toward his cabinet.

"I think we have some medicine in the cabinet here. As for the washcloth, I don't know if you want it...it's been used a bunch."

Gross. I definitely didn't want to know *what* it had been used for. My guess was, though, it had to be for more than just bathing. He was a teenager like me, after all.

"Thanks so much!" I called, pulling open his cabinet with a quick yank and opening all of his bags. Suitcase - no passport. Gym bag - no passport. Backpack - BINGO. I took the passport and pocketed it into my back jeans. Now for some South Korean merchandise.

At that moment, the guy stuck his head out of the bathroom. "Um, what are you doing?!"

When I heard the shrillness of his voice, I tried my best to slow my breathing. "Just wanted to look at your South Korean jerseys. They're so nice. Same color as ours..." I let my words trail off, turning to face him. I silently prayed that he hadn't seen his passport sticking out of my back pocket.

The smile on his face told me he hadn't, thank God. "Uh-huh. Well, you can look at something else I have that's South Korean and is *underneath* those jerseys once you feel better." This guy just *did not* give up!

"Heh, thanks. I can't wait. Just gotta get that medicine and I'll be good to go!" I clapped my hands together.

"Yeah, about that, we only have aspirin. Does that work?" he raised his eyebrows, licking his lips.

Ugh. I must've been a prized turkey or something to him. I *had* to get this gear and get out of here!

"Sure, that's good." I nodded my head vigorously, hoping that my response would push him back into the bathroom one more time and allow me to get his stuff and get out of here.

The guy disappeared back into the bathroom and I turned back toward the cabinet in a flash, grabbing two South Korean team jerseys and a jacket. Running toward the door, I pulled it open and didn't even bother closing it. I ran like running was my first sport toward my room, where I would stash the goodies until tonight. Until I could see Jae Sung and give them to him. Then, tomorrow, we would go to the American Embassy. *This was it.*

CHAPTER THIRTY-FOUR

Jae Sung (재성)

The nighttime air was cold and wet today. The rain was steadily falling, and I wondered if this was a clue that I would have an upcoming demise. An ominous warning.

I sat on the couch, looking out over the city lights that surrounded the Olympic Village. Sounds of cars honking and people laughing in the village courtyard below wafted up to the rooftop. As I listened, I pondered if this is what it would be like in America or not.

I heard the rooftop door swing open with a creak, and Sloane came over to sit beside me on the couch. She set the South Korean jersey and jacket down next to her, then buried her face against my chest as I took her into my arms.

"I did it. It was pretty easy, actually. That guy was so gullible, and he deserved it. He was such a jerk," she gushed, speaking rapidly.

"What is a *jerk?*" I asked her, giving her sweet little mouth a gentle kiss before sliding backward and leaning against the armrest.

"Not a nice guy."

Anger simmered beneath the surface of my thoughts. Did he hurt her in some way? I would kill him.

"What happened?" I asked instead, trying my best to hide the sudden fear I felt.

"He kissed me, of course, and made comments about how he thought I might be on my...woman thing," she confided in me, her cheeks blazing bright pink. "I just couldn't wait to get out of there."

Guilt flooded my heart, and I immediately questioned if this was the right way to go about all of this. Gathering her hands in mine, I whispered, "I'm sorry I put you through that. Maybe there's another way?"

She shook her head adamantly at me. "No going back now. What's done is done. While I'm sure that this guy will notice his missing jerseys, let's just pray that he doesn't figure out that his passport is gone."

Sloane pulled the green passport out from her back pocket, placing it in the palm of my hands. I turned it over so that I could read the front. "대한민국 (*Daehanmingug* – Republic of Korea)."
Not the "조선민주주의인민공화국 (*Chosŏn Minjujuŭi Inmin Konghwaguk,* Democratic People's Republic of Korea.). Unlike the South Korean passport, mine was a navy blue.

I swallowed the lump in my throat and again turned toward the city, gazing longingly out over it. "You do not know what this means to me. If I could be free, it would be great. But I am worried about my family. If I leave them, they may be put to death or put in a camp. Do you think there is a chance that they will join me later?"

My girlfriend rubbed my arm silently, taking a moment to think this over. It was obvious she did not know the answer, and neither did I. Was I willing to risk my family's life just so I could taste liberty? My heart was torn between love for my family and the desire to be able to make my own choices and live my own life.

Without saying a word, Sloane pulled out her phone and started typing on it. I peered over her shoulder to see what she was writing and saw that she was using her search engine (something called Google) to search for something. I read the words as she typed them out: *How can North Koreans defect to America?*

"Defect. What does that word mean?"

"Basically, it means to escape," she responded, clicking on the first article that came up.

The story was about a woman who left North Korea through China in order to reach South Korea, then eventually the United States. It took this woman two months to safely get through China to Nepal, and another three years to get to South Korea. Once in South Korea, this woman was interrogated by the National Intelligence Service to make sure she was not a spy. Then, she was put in something called a *Hanawon*, or a Settlement Support Center. My fellow countrywoman was taught how to use something called an ATM, how to ride on a train called a subway, and how to use a cell phone. She was put through physical exams and counseling. Daily, she and another group of North Koreans traveled to the grocery store and other everyday places in South Korea in order to familiarize themselves with life outside of the North. Finally, after twelve weeks, the woman and those who came into the center at the same time with her were given eight million Korean won, a home to live in and South Korean citizenship. For a year, this woman lived and worked various, menial jobs in South Korea, saving up so she could come to America. She then applied for an American visitor's visa, was approved after another year, then made her way to the United States. All in all, it took this North Korean defector over five years to come to America.

Wow. This was so crazy. Would it take *me* that long to get to America? What about my family? Maybe this was not such a good idea.

I thought about the life I had waiting for me back in Pyongyang. A good university, my parents and my sister, my halemoni were all waiting for me upon my return. What else was waiting for me? Not as much food as I had been able to eat while at the Olympics, that was for sure. The ability to see whom I wanted to when I wanted to? That would be gone as well. Hiding my laptop and my phone would be something I would have to keep doing. I do not want that life anymore. Since coming to Beijing, something had changed in me. I had changed. I wanted to be free, and I knew that I could not be the only North Korean who thought this way.

"It seems very hard, but I can do it. My only question is — when will I see you? Will it be years before I see you again?" I cupped Sloane's face in my hands, staring into her bright blue eyes.

"That *will* be extremely difficult. I can't imagine not seeing you for a day," Sloane replied, leaning up to place a soft kiss on my forehead. Her lips felt like honey on my skin.

"Even so, we must try. I do not want to go back to my life in North Korea. It is too difficult there. I will get to America, no matter how long it takes me, and I will immediately come to see you," I promised her, even as I was unsure if this was a possible feat to accomplish.

"Whatever it takes," Sloane whispered to me, wrapping her arms around my torso and resting her head on my shoulder.

As I hugged her back, I breathed, "Whatever it takes."

CHAPTER THIRTY-FIVE

Sloane

The next morning, I waited in the courtyard for Jae Sung to meet me, my thoughts bouncing around with nerves in my mind. This was it. The day. Would this plan work? We were about to find out.

Jae Sung and I agreed to meet at noon and we would walk right out of the gate and try to catch a cab to the American Embassy. He would be changing into his South Korean jersey and jacket in the bathroom of the lobby, throwing his North Korean team outfit in the trash. This was all so risky and the chance of getting caught was high. I wondered if this would work, but I reminded myself that it was worth the risk.

If *he* got caught, it might mean certain death.

What about if *I* got caught? Could I lose my citizenship? I had never thought about that until now. This morning, I researched China's stance on North Korea on my phone and discovered that if a North Korean is found in China, they are sent back to North Korea immediately. What about the Americans helping North Koreans, though?

Surprisingly, I couldn't find a single article about that, but judging by China's stance on North Korea, I am sure it wouldn't be good.

At that moment, I saw Jae Sung exiting our dormitory doors, a gym bag slung over his shoulder. He headed toward me swiftly, taking on a different walk altogether. When we met, even though I wanted to reach out and grab his hand, I didn't. He didn't reach for me either. It was best to keep it that way until we were alone – no use in bringing more attention to ourselves, because there were other athletes and coaches and Olympics personnel milling about around us.

"How do you feel?" I asked him, peering up into his face.

"Not well. It must have been the Chinese chicken I had last night in the cafeteria," he joked, giving me a small wink.

I laughed along with him as we turned and started making our way toward the gates. "You aren't alone. We're together, and we can do this. Do you have the passport?"

Jae Sung patted an invisible pocket on the inside of the South Korean team jacket. "Right here."

It occurred to me then that maybe we would be in trouble for taking someone's passport. If we could explain the situation, though, maybe the embassy workers would understand and the douche would get his passport back. I silently prayed to the higher powers for some grace and compassion on the part of the embassy.

"What do you have in the bag?" I asked, peering at it with curiosity filling my every pore.

"An extra change of clothes, my *real* passport, my illegal phone…" he listed off items. We turned and made our way to the gate.

Just as we got there, I heard a commotion taking place in the courtyard. "Hey you! Stop! That's my jersey and my shirt!" Oh no…Mr. Douche was chasing us!

Jae Sung and I immediately sprang into a sprint, running out through the Olympic Village gates and toward the taxi waiting area. He pulled open the door of the nearest taxi and we both jumped in. "American Embassy," I requested, swallowing down the fear that was rising in the form of bile in my throat.

We made it just in time, because Mr. Douche approached our taxi right as we drove off! I looked back and locked eyes with the guy whose passport and outfits we stole and felt a tiny bit of guilt rip through me. Shaking it off, I turned back around in my seat and leaned on Jae Sung.

"One step down, a few more to go," I whispered in his ear.

The taxi driver peered back at us. "Olympics huh? Are you two athletes?"

"Yes," we both replied in unison, looking over at each other with a smile.

When we got to the embassy, there were a ton of people skirting the exterior walls. They were holding signs and chanting, "Freedom for North Korea!"

Jae Sung and I looked at each other in fear.

We were both thinking the same thing: Would anyone from this crowd be able to recognize him as a North Korean instead of a South Korean?

I thanked the taxi driver and handed over thirty-three Chinese won (the equivalent of five American dollars) for the ride. Jae Sung and I slipped out of the taxi and made our way gingerly up to the gate of the embassy. Standing at the post of the embassy were both an American soldier and a Chinese one, staring silently into each other's eyes as if daring each other to blink.

"May we go in?" Jae Sung asked, flashing his South Korean passport. I took my own passport out and showed it to them as well.

The Chinese soldier said nothing but pointed to a small window next to the gate, which an embassy worker hid behind in a room attached to the gate. Jae Sung and I turned toward the window and approached it. Apprehension tugged at every nerve ending in my body.

"Good afternoon," I greeted the woman, whose shiny brown eyes greeted my blue ones back. "We're here to see the visa department."

I had done some research on the American Embassy before we made it there. Also, I had requested an appointment at 12:30 p.m. with them. I was so glad I had because the first words out of the woman's mouth was: "Appointment?"

Jae Sung turned to look at me, his mouth wide open in fear, and before he could respond, I affirmed, "Yes. 12:30 p.m.."

He reached over to silently thank me by squeezing my hand. Another hurtle down, maybe a million more to go.

"Name?" The woman peered down at her computer, poised to type. I gave the woman both my name and the name on the passport (Chan Yeol Lee), and she began entering the information into her computer. "Got you right here."

The worker printed out a ticket of some sort and handed it to us. "Take this to the soldiers over there and they will let you in."

We both thanked her, then headed back over to the soldiers. Silently, I handed the American soldier the ticket. He studied it for just a brief second, then handed it back to me. "Go in."

Taking my hand, Jae Sung led me up to the doors and we entered. The first thing I noticed was the metal detector.

"It's a good thing we didn't bring our gold medals," I quipped, squeezing his hand in solidarity.

Jae Sung didn't laugh back, though. His face remained stoic as we approached the metal detector and put our bags on the conveyor belt, then turned and walked through the detectors. An embassy worker waved us with a wand for extra security.

"Purpose here?" a Chinese security guard queried us as we collected our things.

"We are applying for a visa to America," I replied, trying to keep my voice nonchalant as if this was an everyday event for me.

"Passports?" he kept going, eyeing us suspiciously.

Jae Sung took out the South Korean passport, I took out my American one, and we handed them both over for inspection. The guard easily passed mine back to me but he looked Jae Sung up and down as he studied the South Korean passport as well.

I forced myself to calm down, breathing deeply as inconspicuous as I could. Would we make it through?

After another moment (which felt like one hundred years), the man handed Jae Sung back his fake passport. I tried not to let him hear me blow out a breath by turning my head and pretending to cough into my elbow.

"Thank you," we both chimed, then took each other's hands.

"You are welcome. Second floor," the security guard replied, still training his eyes on us.

Jae Sung and I made our way to a set of silver elevator doors, and I pushed the up button. As we waited, we exchanged a smile. One more milestone was complete, only a few more steps to go.

When we were safe in the elevator, Jae Sung pulled me into a hug. "Thank you for doing this with me."

"You're welcome," I replied, nuzzling my head into his chest. "We're almost there. This has been cra—"

The elevator doors opened with a *ding*, interrupting our sweet little juncture. He and I broke apart abruptly and exited, immediately searching for the door to the visa department.

This would be the last step we would need to take before Jae Sung could announce that he was a "North Korean defector looking for asylum in America."

The door was at the end of a long hallway. It beamed at us as if it was made from the same gold we both achieved at the Olympics. Almost home.

As we reached the door, Jae Sung turned toward me and gave me one last hug. "No matter what, I want you to know that.. that...I am thankful for you."

My heart was inundated with gratitude as well. "I'm thankful for you as well. You have already changed my life in the span of a few weeks."

Jae Sung took a deep breath in and I knew he wasn't done telling me whatever he needed to say. "Also, I want to let you know...I am...what do you Americans say?...Falling for you."

The smile that broke across my face was involuntary and I hugged him again, crushing his body to mine. I couldn't help it – it was a natural response from me at this moment. Joy.

"I think...I'm falling for you too," I whispered, leaning back to look into his eyes.

We smiled at each other, then Jae Sung pulled the door open, and we entered the visa reception area.

CHAPTER THIRTY-SIX

Jae Sung (재성)

Here we were. The lobby for the visa department at the American Embassy. What would happen next? I did not know. What I knew was that Americans do not turn away North Korean defectors. I was safe in this room.

"May I help you?" a woman called out from behind the front desk, which was shrouded with a wall and a window. Next to her window was a door, which I thought might lead to something called the consulate's office.

"Yes, we are here for an appointment at 12:30 p.m. with the visa department," Sloane answered for us both, stepping up to the window. I followed her, eager to get to the next part of our journey.

"Awesome. It will be with the consulate," the woman answered. I glanced at her nametag to get her name. Nancy.

"Thank you, Nancy," I replied, shifting from foot-to-foot, unable to hide my anticipation at this point.

"You're welcome," she answered me, giving me a warm smile. "South Korea, huh? You guys must be here for the Olympics."

"Yes, we're both swimmers," Sloane informed her, signing her name on the sign-in sheet on the clipboard.

"That's so wonderful. How did you do?" Nancy engaged us, peering up at us with hope stretched across her face.

"We both won gold," I told her, thinking to myself, *Only, I won it for North Korea.*

I had left my medal behind. After so many years of working hard to win that object, I had to leave it in China. My efforts seemed pointless at this moment, but in light of what I was gaining, it seemed irrelevant now. In just a short amount of time, my goals and desires had changed completely. It was like I was a different person altogether.

Sloane and I chose a seat near the door to the inner office, and I looked over at the magazines on the side table. One called *Vogue* displayed a woman with so much makeup on her face that she looked like a doll. In North Korea, the only magazines we have display the leaders of our country and talk about the work that the government is doing. This one looked like it was for pleasure.

Amazing!

The door swung open and a hefty man in a tailored gray suit came out to meet us. "Sloane, Chan Yeol?" he asked.

We both nodded. "Yes, sir," Sloane responded, standing up to greet him with a handshake. I stood up and shook the man's hand as well.

"Dan Puccata, Ambassador to the United States," the man informed us, leading us back into an office that overlooked the city with floor-to-ceiling windows.

Sloane and I exchanged wide-eyed looks.

Wow. The ambassador.

Once the door was closed, I opened my mouth to speak the first truth that I had spoken since arriving at the United States embassy. This was it.

The time for transparency was now.

"My real name is Jae Sung Kim, and I am a North Korean. I am seeking asylum in the United States."

CHAPTER THIRTY-SEVEN

Sloane

You could have heard a pin drop in the room. Ambassador Puccata stared at us for what felt like an eternity, studying every feature of our faces. Then, he let out a hearty laugh.

"Son, I would like to ask how you got up here, but the first thing I need to do is ask for your *actual* passport to confirm your real identity," he spoke, his voice taking on a warm tone.

Jae Sung reached into his gym bag and pulled out his North Korean passport. He hesitated for a moment, looking down at it, then cautiously handed it over to the ambassador.

I leaned over and grabbed his hand, knowing we were safe to show some affection in this room.

Ambassador Puccata seemed like he was on our side, at least. Who would address someone as *son* if they were angry at them?

The Ambassador studied the passport for a bit, flipping through its pages to look at the visa to China that Jae Sung had, which happened to be his only stamp.

"I take it you are both athletes," Ambassador Puccata surmised, handing Jae Sung back his passport.

My boyfriend and I both let out breaths. I don't think either of us knew we were holding in air. "Yes," I answered him. "Swimmers, to be exact."

"Is that how you met?" the Ambassador questioned us, walking over to a cabinet and pulling out some forms. He came back over to us, sat down, and placed them in front of us on the desk.

I studied the titles of two of them. *Immigrant Visa Application* and *Refugee Application*.

This was it. It was working. Jae Sung is coming to America!

For the next few hours, Jae Sung and I filled in the ambassador on our relationship and answered any questions he had about us. He had a lot of them, actually. Jae Sung filled out the paperwork, surrendered the South Korean passport, and took pictures for a visa.

The whole process was extremely exhausting. I could see myself taking a nap on the nice, black leather couch the ambassador had in his office…if he would let me, of course.

"The process for you to enter America will take a few years, I hope you know," Ambassador Puccata enlightened us with even more information. "Jae Sung, you will have to go to South Korea first in order to get reeducated. Have you learned about that process?"

Jae Sung and I nodded our heads together, signaling that we understood the measures we would have to take in order to finally get him to America.

"Tonight, you will have to stay here, in the embassy, for protection," Ambassador Puccata continued, leaning back in his black leather office chair and keeping his eyes fixed on us. "Sloane, you will need to return to the Olympic village. I'm sure your teammates and coach are wondering where you are."

Disappointment coursed through my heart and mind. I wanted to stay with Jae Sung, actually, but I quickly reminded myself that this would have to be what it would be so that we could get him to the United States. *This is good-bye, Sloane.*

Ambassador Puccata stood up, shaking both of our hands in his large but smooth right hand. "You will get your visa to South Korea in a few days, Jae Sung."

Jae Sung nodded. "Yes sir. But…when will I see Sloane again?"

The ambassador chuckled. "That, I don't know my boy. What I do know is that you will be free. I'm glad you were able to make your way here safely."

"We are too," I agreed with the ambassador. "Thank you."

Ambassador Puccata walked us toward another door to the left of his office. "We are going to take a different route instead. It will take us to the place where the North Korean defectors stay while they wait to go to South Korea. Sloane, you can exit through the stairs there."

Before we exited the ambassador's office, I turned to Jae Sung. "Here's my number and email address," I offered, handing him a piece of paper. "I wrote it down last night because I didn't know if we would get separated or not."

Jae Sung nodded solemnly, his eyes trained on mine. "Sloane, is this good-bye?" I thought I caught a single tear forming in the corner of his left eye.

"Not good-bye. Just see you soon, babe," I answered him, not caring at all if the ambassador heard me use that term of endearment.

CHAPTER THIRTY-EIGHT

Jae Sung (재성)

After Sloane exited through the stairs, the ambassador finished taking me room by room, showing me the computer area, the library, and finally, the bedrooms. Another North Korean was perched on the top bunk of a bunk bed, reading a book. When we entered the room, he sat up straight, his eyes alert and fixed on the ambassador and me.

"Good afternoon, Sung Ho," Ambassador Puccata greeted the boy, who looked to be even younger than myself. My guess was he was about fourteen or fifteen. "Sung Ho has been here two days. He came by nighttime with the help of a non-profit organization."

I was so glad that I was not alone in this room or this next step of my journey. My halemoni's God had provided me with a friend, one who could speak my language and understand all of my feelings.

"*Annyunghasaeyeo*," I greeted Sung Ho loosely, bowing my head even though I was clearly older than him.

He returned the greeting, then went back to reading his book, sneaking curious glances at me.

"I'll leave you here, Jae Sung. Someone will come to get you for meal times, just to be safe. There's a restroom over there. Your visa will be brought to you when it is ready. You're welcome to use the facilities in this area, but *do not leave this area. I repeat — do not leave this location.*"

"Yes sir." I gulped down an invisible mass of anxiety in the back of my mouth and felt it land with a *thud* in the pit of my stomach, not willing to leave me. My hands sweated involuntarily as I made my way toward the bottom bunk beneath Sung Ho.

The ambassador gave me a little wave, then turned and left the room. I let out a giant sigh that I had been holding in for what felt like forever.

"You are not South Korean," Sung Ho spoke to me in our native tongue with a sheepish look on his face. "Did you steal that?"

"Yeah, I did what I had to do in order to get here," I replied, looking up at him with a semi-embarrassed smile.

"Me too," he confirmed, putting his book down and leaning over the railing to get closer to me. "I came in the middle of the night and met a missionary couple at the river. They hid me in China for two weeks and fed me a bunch of food before bringing me to the embassy with a fake South Korean visa."

Even though Sung Ho was eager to exchange stories, I chose not to give anymore information about my journey. Who knew if he was a spy, as Sloane said, were in other countries, especially those in Asia.

I leaned back on my pillows, tuning out Sung Ho, and thought of Sloane. She would be making her way back to the Olympic Village right now. Alone. Without me. Would Chan Yeol harass her? Would she be okay?

Exhaustion suddenly flooded my body, and I realized how truly tired I was. Shutting my eyes, I easily fell asleep, lulled into slumber by the gentle hum of the air conditioner, free at last.

———◇———

Sloane and I talked every day on the phone, courtesy of the American Embassy. She had gone back to the village, somehow successfully avoiding Chan Yeol at whatever cost. His passport had been returned to him by the American Embassy, with a note on it that stated, "Found in the courtyard at the Olympic Village." Somehow, I guessed that Ambassador Puccata had done something to make this happen.

Within a couple of weeks, Sloane was returning to America. She told me how excited she was to see her parents and return to "everyday life," but that she missed me so much. My heart was broken in two when I heard her state that sentiment. I told her how much I missed her as well and could not wait to be with her again.

Dinner came every day at 6:30 p.m. It was usually the same – pasta, pizza, what I surmised had to be American food because we did not eat this type of food in North Korea very much. My visa came within a few days, as the ambassador had promised me, and I prepared to go to South Korea.

My parents and I talked on a secret phone line that the American Embassy set up. I was surprised to hear them admit that they were afraid for me, since I had never heard them talk like this before. I reassured them that all would be okay and once I was in America, I would work on bringing them there as well. I asked them if anyone had asked where I was, and they responded that there had been a lot of questioning from the police in Pyongyang, to which they replied that the Dear Leader had sent me to work on something on behalf of our country in Beijing. Even so, the policemen and women kept coming daily, badgering my parents with queries about me. This worried me, but I knew I was powerless to help them at the moment. All I could do was pray that my eomma, abba, Jjamae, and halmeoni would be okay.

Sung Ho left way before I did – a few weeks, to be exact. He was talking a mile a minute about how excited he was to meet some South Korean girls. I just listened and allowed the little guy to rant. Every North Korean has their own dreams of what freedom looks like. Then again, I was with Sloane, and Sung Ho would have a South Korean girl for sure.

Eventually, I was allowed to leave the embassy in order to go to the airport. In just a few hours, I would board a plane bound for Seoul. I milled around in the airport, feeling lonely but excited to see what an airport looked like. The architecture of the Beijing Capital International Airport was artistic and sophisticated, and it looked like the government had put a lot of money into it. People from everywhere walked around, and I took in all of the different dialects, accents, and languages.

With the money provided from the embassy, I bought myself a sandwich at some restaurant that I had never heard of before called Subway. I bit into the sandwich and my tastebuds danced around with the delectable meat and cheese and vegetables I was consuming. Their slogan was *Eat fresh*, and I had never tasted more fresh food in my life...except for at the Olympic Village.

"北京首都国际机场所有旅客请注意。飞往韩国首尔的727航班正在登机。再次，在 12 号登机口乘坐 727 航班飞往韩国首尔."

"Attention all passengers in the Beijing Capital International Airport. Flight 727 to Seoul, South Korea is boarding. Again, Flight 727 to Seoul, South Korea at gate 12."

I threw my trash away hastily and walked toward the gate, feeling every bit of the extra ten pounds I had put on since arriving at the American Embassy.

As I boarded the plane, I took one last look out the floor-to-ceiling windows at Beijing. This was the last time I would probably see this city.

Even though I searched for images of Seoul while at the embassy, I still wondered what that city was *really* like.

When I arrived, I would follow the process of the woman Sloane and I had read about a few weeks back on the rooftop of the Olympic Village. According to the American Embassy workers, when I landed at the airport, someone from the Settlement Support Center would pick me up and take me to the center. There, I would be given twelve weeks of classes and excursions around the city. After my time there, I would be given a job, apartment, and money. The process seemed simple, but judging by my time up until now, I knew it was anything but that.

Just as I settled back in my seat, ready to strap myself in, my phone vibrated in my front pocket. I reached in, frustrated with myself that I had not turned it off, and saw that it was Sloane. My heart soared with happiness in my chest.

"Sloane, I just boarded," I informed my girlfriend, waiting for her response.

"That's so great!" she cried over the noises around her.

"Where are you right now?" I closed my eyes, trying to envision what she was seeing so many miles away.

"A coffee shop, studying for an exam," she let me know in response.

"Nice," I replied, thinking of coffee. That was one thing I had forgotten to get at the airport. A nice little nap would do, though.

"I'm so excited for you, babe! You did it! You're free!" she exclaimed, and I wondered who was around her to hear that. Oh well. No hiding this all now...except from the Chinese government, of course.

We were interrupted by an Air Korea flight attendant leaning over me. "Sir, it is time to turn off the phone and strap your seatbelt. We were about ready for take off."

I nodded my head at her, putting my phone between my cheek and my shoulder so that I could strap my seatbelt. "Sloane, I have to go, but I will call you when I land in Seoul."

I could almost hear my girlfriend nod through the phone. We had begun to know each other's mannerisms so well.

"I wish I could send you a care package," she joked, humor lighting up her voice. "It would say on the outside: 'Welcome to South Korea, babe.'"

I laughed and told her, "Good luck studying on your exam. You got this!"

We hung up and I leaned back in my seat, closing my eyes, readying myself for a nap.

All of this happened because I met a girl who opened my eyes to my situation. All of this occurred because I found out that I did not have to live unfree. All of this was worth it.

Jae Sung (재성)
Four Years Later

"Ladies and gentlemen, we are about to make our descent into Barnstable Municipal Airport. Welcome to Cape Cod, Massachusetts," the pilot announced over the loudspeaker as our plane began to show signs of slowing down.

I took a deep breath and looked out the window at the fields that surrounded us. The area was sparse and I wondered what Cape Cod looked like.

After arriving in South Korea, I went through what was called The Reunification Process. When I exited the center, I secured a job as a dishwasher at a local restaurant, which was something I never thought I would do. However, I quickly learned that any job is worth taking. After working that job for a while, I became a server, then a manager of the restaurant. I used every work ethic my parents taught me in order to make them proud, even from afar.

My parents and I spoke every night on a secret telephone provided by the center. They informed me that the police had eventually dropped off their case, which I counted as a miracle.

My halemoni was still in good spirits, even at the age of ninety-four, and my sister was going on to college at Kim Il Sung University. All was well…for now.

Once I worked for about a year, Ambassador Puccata sent a visa request to the American Embassy in Seoul on my behalf. It was for a student visa for four years. He informed me that I could study, then try to get a job and remain in the United States on a work visa. I stayed in touch with the ambassador while I lived and worked in South Korea.

Finally, after three years, my visa came, and I was able to pick it up at the American Embassy in Jongnogu, Seoul. This embassy was manned by South Korean and American soldiers and was a little easier to get into this time, since I was now a South Korean citizen.

I applied to Bridgewater State University in Cape Cod, set to major in International Affairs. It was the university that was the closest to Sloane's new home. She had graduated just a few weeks prior to me with a bachelor's degree in International Affairs and would be working in the US Customs Service in Boston.

Within a few weeks, I booked my flight to Cape Cod, eager to see my girlfriend and her home country, which was to be my home country without a doubt one day.

"Sir, you can get up now," a flight attendant informed me, peering down at me with concern.

I had not realized that I was lost in my thoughts. "Oh, sorry." As I hurried to get my bag, I noticed that everyone was off the plane…except for me. Had I really been *that* deep in my thoughts?

Wow.

Exiting the plane, I entered the terminal. It was flooded with natural light from its floor-to-ceiling windows. This airport was a little smaller than the ones I had encountered in Beijing and Seoul, but it was nice and neat, and not as crowded.

First, I had to go to baggage claim, then, I would see my sweetheart for the first time in about four and a half years. *To think, this all started on a rooftop in Beijing...*

Sloane
Four years later

My parents and I stood side by side with our signs for Jae Sung in our hands. "Welcome to America!" and "*Annyunghaseyeo*, Jae Sung!" were written on them in our best handwriting.

The anticipation was killing me! It felt like it had taken forever for him to get here...well, it actually had. Four years wasn't an overnight matter.

After I returned to the safety of America, I let my parents know the whole story about Jae Sung. Naturally, they were a little upset with me, but it was more out of concern than anger. Then, it turned to concern for him. Some days, I felt like they liked him more than me, especially when they talked on the phone. That was okay with me, though. He needed a set of parents who could help him when he would arrive in this country for the first time.

Just then, I saw a familiar face and body come around the corner. I dropped my sign and ran to him, not caring who saw or judged me for my erratic behavior. Jae Sung dropped his bag as well, hurrying toward me and picking me up. I threw my arms around his neck and smothered him with kisses, my desire for him growing.

"I'm here! I finally made it, babe!" He placed me back on the floor but didn't let go of me, his hands resting at my sides.

"You made it, baby, you made it," was all I could manage to say as surprising tears flowed down both of my cheeks.

Smoothly, Jae Sung wiped the tears from my face and kissed each cheek. "I am so happy to see you. It feels like the first time all over again."

My dad cleared his throat and said, "Sorry to interrupt the two lovebirds, but I would like to meet my future son-in-law."

"Daaaaad!" I squealed, feeling like I was eighteen again.

Jae Sung smiled at me and replied with a bit of joy in his voice, referring to himself in third person, "He's right here." My eyes grew wide, but my heart confirmed that I was happy at this admonishment.

He extended his hand to my dad in order to shake it, but my dad pulled him into a big bear hug instead. My mom followed suit, kissing his cheek. They both handed them the signs we had made and he looked them over, chuckling to himself.

"I love this," he admitted, "But most of all, I'm just so happy to be here. With all of you."

"We are happy too," my mom gushed, reaching over and squeezing his hand lightly. "Let's get your bags, son."

We both followed my parents toward the baggage carousels, taking each other's hands and squeezing hard. It was like we must have both thought that Jae Sung would disappear or be whisked away by North Korean or Chinese guards. But here...we were free.

As we stood waiting for the luggage, Jae Sung leaned over to whisper something in my ear, "Sloane...I love you."

It was the first time I had heard those words from him, even though I had felt them for so long. I thought that maybe he had felt them too, but I was too scared to be the first person to say them to him.

"I love you too," I acknowledged my own feelings, caressing his hand with mine.

We had our whole lives ahead of us. The next task would be to find a way to help Jae Sung's family escape North Korea and come to America.

And to think, this all started on a rooftop in Beijing...

Real Newspapers
from 2008

Editions ENGLISH ∨

THE DONG-A ILBO

Headline News   Business   National   Politics   International   Sports   Culture   Editorial   Op-ed

Defector returns to North Korea for the sake of her son

Posted July. 02, 2012 00:58,

◀)) A- A+ 한국어 f 🐦

A North Korean defector who returned to the Stalinist country and held a news conference Pyongyang Thursday was found to have returned to North Korea to save her son and daughter-in-law, who were forced to move to a mountainous village.

According to the essays, diary and photos of Park In-suk exclusively obtained by The Dong-A Ilbo on Friday, Park was upset over her son's fate and considered returning to North Korea from 2010. She showed feelings of guilt toward her son in her essays and diary.

Please forgive my life in which I have sinned against you (her son). I intended to resolve financial matters by meeting my father in China, but I ended up losing my reason and came to (the South)...abandoning my family, Park said.

I have ruined my son. I feel sorry for the parents of my daughter-

Headline News

Yoon considers holding the ROK-US-Japan NATO Summit

Hyundai Steel develops alloy steel for EV gear speed reducers

Telephone booths transformed into battery stations for electric motorcycles

Biden's Uyghur labor law may affect Korean importers

New photo shows Woods' injured right leg without leg sleeve

Work Cited: The Dong-A Ilbo. "Defector Returns to North Korea for the Sake of Her Son." *Defector returns to North Korea for the sake of her son* [Seoul], 2 July 2012, https://www.donga.com/en/article/all/20120702/4041 63/1. Accessed 21 June 2022.

Works Cited: Chun, Susan. "Radio gives hope to North and South Koreans." *CNN*, 27 February 2008, http://www.cnn.com/2008/WORLD/asiapcf/02/27/ch o.dissidentradio/index.html. Accessed 21 June 2022.

Work Cited: Olympic Games. "North Korea at the Beijing 2008 Olympic Games." *Olympian Database*, 2008, https://www.olympiandatabase.com/index.php?id=11 9224&L=1. Accessed 21 June 2022.

On a Rooftop in Beijing Playlist

All of these songs are South Korean (aka "K-Pop") songs that were popular in 2008. I included them based on the lyrics, which I think match the relationship that Sloane and Jae Sung have.

Artist	Song
Crown J (featuring Seo In Young)	"Too Much"
Mighty Mouth (featuring Yoon Eun Hye)	"Saranghe"
J-Walk (featuring Eun Ji Won)	"My Love"
Kim Jong Kook	"Today More than Yesterday"
SS501	"Déjà vu"
SS501	"Find"
Shinhwa	"Just One More Time"
Alex	"If It's You"
Nell	"Time Spent Walking Through Memories"
SNSD (Girl's Generation)	"Kissing You"
DBSK	"Picture of You"
SHINee	"Romantic"
BigBang	"Make Love"
Wonder Girls	"Nobody"
DBSK	"Mirotic"

Acknowledgements

First, I want to thank my readers of *On a Rooftop in Beijing*. I hope that you found this book to be eye-opening, thought-provoking, and thrilling.

Also, I would like to say thank you to the North Korean refugees as well as the churches that helped the refugees that I worked with in South Korea. Without you, this book would not be here. Thank you for opening *my* eyes to the plight of the North Koreans in such a profound way that it changed my life and my purpose.

To my beta readers J.R, Nicole, Leslie, Ashley, Lekha, Bri: I appreciate the time and effort you put into reading this book with a critical eye so that it could reach its full potential. You made *On a Rooftop in Beijing* (and my writing style) better overall.

Muse Literary: You have been so wonderful to work with and I am grateful for all of the work you have done for me and my book. I look forward to hopefully working with you in the future.

Lastly, I would like to say thank you to God, for without Him, I wouldn't have traveled to South Korea and this book (as well as my life's purpose) would never have been possible.

About the Author

Maggie Paredes lives in Orlando, Florida with her two dogs and her music producer/professor husband, J.R. By day, she is an elementary school teacher, and by night, she reads like it's her second job. Maggie's travels abroad to Japan, Mexico, Spain, and India, as well as her two years living in South Korea (including her work with North Korean refugees while there), inspired this story. *On a Rooftop in Beijing* is her first book.

CPSIA information can be obtained
at www.ICGtesting.com
Printed in the USA
LVHW020722120423
744094LV00001B/14

9 781958 714355